FUGITIVE MANHUNT

SHAREE STOVER

LOVE INSPIRED SUSPENSE
INSPIRATIONAL ROMANCE

Special thanks and acknowledgment are given to Sharee Stover for her contribution to the Colorado K-9 Unit miniseries.

PLEASE RECYCLE · THIS PRODUCT IS RECYCLABLE

Recycling programs for this product may not exist in your area.

ISBN-13: 978-1-335-91904-5

Fugitive Manhunt

For questions and comments about the quality of this book, please contact us at CustomerService@Harlequin.com.

Love Inspired
22 Adelaide St. West, 41st Floor
Toronto, Ontario M5H 4E3, Canada
www.LoveInspired.com

HarperCollins Publishers
Macken House, 39/40 Mayor Street Upper,
Dublin 1, D01 C9W8, Ireland
www.HarperCollins.com

Printed in Lithuania

1 2 3 4 5 6 7 8 9 10 LIT 28 27 26 25

The kidnapper needed her alive.

As bait? Or worse?

Then in the distance, Lizzie heard the promise of help. A bark.

Lizzie squeezed her eyes shut, silently begging God to lead her K-9 to her.

The man cursed under his breath, confirming she hadn't imagined her partner's barking. She couldn't let him take her away. Whatever he had planned for Lizzie terrified her.

Another yelp. Reena.

"Lizzie!" Walker's voice.

With another curse, the man dropped her, and half her body splashed into cold water. The startling chill of the creek caught her off guard.

The assailant sent a swift kick to her side that shot horrendous pain through her.

She sucked in an excruciating breath, tucking her hands against her chest...then braced for another hit.

* * *

COLORADO K-9 UNIT

Searching for the Truth by Laura Scott
Tracking the Taken Child by Sharon Dunn
Danger in the Rockies by Terri Reed
Protecting the Baby by Jodie Bailey
Fugitive Manhunt by Sharee Stover
Hunting an Arsonist by Jessica R. Patch
Uncovering Explosive Secrets by Maggie K. Black
Unraveling a Crime Ring by Valerie Hansen
Christmas K-9 Security by Lynette Eason & Lenora Worth

Colorado native **Sharee Stover** lives in the Midwest with her real-life-hero husband, youngest child and her obnoxiously lovable German shepherd. A self-proclaimed word nerd, she loves the power of words to transform, ignite and restore. She writes Christian romantic suspense combining heart-racing, nail-biting suspense and the delight of falling in love all in one. Connect with her at www.shareestover.com.

Books by Sharee Stover

Love Inspired Suspense

Untraceable Evidence
Grave Christmas Secrets
Cold Case Trail
Tracking Concealed Evidence
Framing the Marshal
Defending the Witness
Seeking Justice
Guarded by the Marshal

Iowa State Troopers

Guarding the Child Witness

Mountain Country K-9 Unit

Her Duty Bound Defender

Dakota K-9 Unit

Deadly Badlands Pursuit

Colorado K-9 Unit

Fugitive Manhunt

Visit the Author Profile page at LoveInspired.com.

He shall call upon me, and I will answer him:
I will be with him in trouble; I will deliver him,
and honour him.

—*Psalms* 91:15

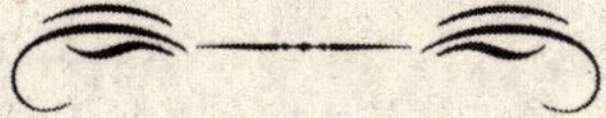

Fugitive Manhunt is for the one who has been running away from themselves.

Come back to the Father, who loves you more than you can ever imagine.

ONE

The brisk August morning and cloudless sky did nothing to alleviate K-9 officer Lizzie Reynolds's dread. She tugged the leash of her partner, golden retriever Reena, and stared up at the Taylor residence, where she'd be conducting this morning's police interview.

"I did not sign up for this task force to be a baby stealer," she told her colleague, Lavender PD K-9 officer Trevor Slate. They convened beside her marked patrol unit, parked on the street.

Trevor jerked his chin. "Neither did I, but if the DNA proves the Taylors bought their six-month-old baby, we've got no choice." He gave a gentle tug of his partner Lark's leash, urging the arson detection dog to his side.

Lizzie had joined the elite Colorado K-9 Unit, a task force comprising K-9 officers from the Denver area, with the intention of taking down a criminal illegal adoption ring. Just the day before, the task force received intel on a Bison Valley couple, Rolf and Marina Taylor, who'd adopted six-month-old Julianna through Family Hope—an online adoption group that paired hopeful parents with children in need.

Although Family Hope appeared legitimate at a glance, its guarded site caused concern when presented against task force tech analyst Eva Gomez's advanced skills, which roused the team's suspicions. Plus, Julianna matched the age and adoption timing of one of the newborn victims on the case.

Lizzie's current assignment required her to interview the young married couple and discern if Julianna might be one of the stolen infants sold on the black market by the illegal adoption ring. The case turned Lizzie's stomach. The task force had been investigating for four months, and thus far, they hadn't identified those responsible for the murders of three teenage mothers and the abduction of their newborns. Worse, those same criminals were selling the stolen babies to the highest bidder. Not to mention the ticking clock that counted down the seconds COK9 had to find and rescue the fourth kidnap victim, pregnant teen Mia Andrews, before she delivered her baby in October.

Though Lizzie was a Bison Valley native, she'd only encountered the Taylors in passing. Still, they were aware she was an officer, which provided her the advantage in requesting the meeting.

"What a way to get to know your neighbors," Lizzie deadpanned.

Trevor offered the hint of a smile, but he appeared distracted.

"Everything okay?" she asked.

"Yeah, just family stuff." He turned away momentarily, adjusting Lark's harness.

Lizzie took the hint and shifted topics. "I want to believe these folks are innocent, but if Julianna turns out to be one of the stolen babies, do you think Rolf and Marina were aware the adoption was illegal?" Lizzie asked, voicing her thoughts aloud.

"I hope not, but it's not inconceivable they knew and chose to look the other way out of desperation," Trevor replied.

That didn't relieve Lizzie's concern and the dread for the task ahead of them. "Let's do this." Lizzie closed her driver's door, and they approached the pristine two-story home with its manicured lawn and flowering bushes perfectly placed in front of the small wooden porch. She inhaled deeply then rang the doorbell.

Marina Taylor answered quickly, no doubt watching for their arrival. Lizzie hoped her attention was due to nervousness rather than guilt. Who wouldn't be apprehensive with two police officers and their K-9s standing outside her front door?

"Good morning. Thanks for agreeing to meet with us." Lizzie offered a warm smile, but Rolf Taylor's suspicion oozed from where he stood, cradling baby Julianna and leaning against the stair railing.

"Sure." Marina's voice quavered, confirming her trepidation. She stepped to the side, permitting the group to enter.

Lizzie didn't miss the flicker of concern that passed between the couple. She moved to the closest seat and monitored Reena for alerts that something was off. Her K-9 appeared disinterested.

Trevor perched on the edge of the matching armchair beside her, picking up on her cues. Both stroked their dogs' necks, attempting to appear casual, though the interview with the Taylors was far from it.

"We appreciate you meeting with us on such short notice," Lizzie said.

Neither Taylor replied.

Rolf stepped forward, gently passing Julianna to Marina as if he didn't want her near the officers. Lizzie maintained a neutral expression when Rolf tossed a file folder on the coffee table a little harder than necessary. "This is the paperwork you requested. It'll prove there's nothing untoward about Julianna's adoption."

Trevor lifted the file, scanning through the documents before handing it to Lizzie. She did the same, scouring for anything suspicious or out of sorts. On paper, everything matched what Eva had discovered about the Taylors, confirming, at least on the surface, that Julianna's adoption was legal. But documents were easily forged. Until they investigated, they wouldn't know for certain.

"Thank you for your cooperation." Lizzie held out the file for Rolf, who snatched it away with vehemence.

"So, we're good?" Marina hugged the baby closer.

"There's one more thing," Lizzie said.

The couples' faces revealed their consternation.

"We anticipated your demands," Rolf replied sourly.

"A DNA sample is necessary to confirm Julianna isn't one of the babies in the illegal adoption ring," Trevor explained.

"But what if she is?" Marina's question was halted by her husband's hand on her arm.

"She's not," he assured.

"The DNA will provide the evidence all of us need," Lizzie replied.

Marina's eyes welled with tears. "Fine, do what you must."

Trevor rose and approached with the DNA testing kit. Marina turned Julianna to face him. Trevor distracted the baby by making silly faces. His efforts proved beneficial when Julianna offered a wide smile. Trevor used the opportunity to perform the buccal swab on the inside of her cheek, gaining him a loud protest from Julianna at the intrusive betrayal.

"It's okay," Marina cooed, gently kissing the infant's feathery hair.

"This is ludicrous," Rolf said, clearly agitated.

Lizzie got up from the chair. "I understand what an inconvenience—"

"Inconvenience?" Rolf roared. "You're threatening to take away our daughter! How long must we live in this nightmare?"

"I'll hand deliver the test," Trevor advised. "We've already requested they expedite it and will be in touch as soon as possible." With a nod, he and Lark headed outside to his unit.

They'd driven separately to allow a divide-and-conquer setup with the interview. Trevor handled the lab work while Lizzie stayed with the couple.

Lizzie didn't move, determined to gain information before leaving the Taylors. She had a feeling they'd not invite her back, so it was now or never.

The couple gave her a dismissive look. "You've spoken to Family Hope, correct?" Marina asked.

Lizzie folded her hands on her lap. "Yes, we're thoroughly examining every avenue."

"We're finished until the test comes back," Rolf said.

"That depends." Lizzie exhaled. "Is there additional information you're willing to provide to assist with the investigation?"

"You mean you want us to help you take away our daughter?" Rolf skewered her with a murderous glare.

It wasn't that Lizzie blamed them for their defensiveness, but her goal was to obtain their cooperation rather than debate. "As I explained yesterday, our team is searching for a pregnant teenager who's in grave danger. As parents, surely you appreciate the urgency and fear her family endures every day she's gone."

Marina's expression softened. "Oh, how awful."

Rolf took a full step back, creating more distance between them. "What's that got to do with us?"

"One thing might lead to another." Lizzie elaborated, "Our team is dedicated to solving the murders of three young mothers whose babies are also missing."

Marina gasped, placing a finger to her lips and snuggling Julianna tighter. "You don't believe—"

"We're looking at adoption facilities." Lizzie paused, studying the couple's reactions.

Rolf took Julianna from Marina's arms and crossed the room, as though staking his claim on the child. His face shone with perspiration, and he spat his next words in a rapid justification. "If there was anything illegal or untoward about the adoption, we wouldn't have known."

"Was this the first agency you'd worked with?" Lizzie asked.

"Yes," Rolf said.

Based on Marina's raised eyebrows and the almost imperceptible shake of her husband's head, Lizzie concluded Rolf had lied. But why? Was he concealing his guilt or trying to protect his family?

"Were you surprised by the expected fees?" Lizzie asked.

Marina's eyes flashed. "We didn't buy our daughter, Officer. Paying for the mother's health costs is normal in these types of arrangements."

"Absolutely," Lizzie assured the mother. "What I meant was, did you have reservations about Family Hope's terms?"

"None at all," Rolf said a little too quickly.

Lizzie feigned forgetfulness. "I don't recall seeing it in the documents, but what amount did Family Hope require?"

Again, the couple exchanged a concerned glance.

"Fifty thousand dollars, which included the facility's adoption filing fees—" Marina said.

"—and our lawyer confirmed that was legal," Rolf blurted.

Julianna mewed and Marina rose. "I don't mean to sound insensitive, but since you've gotten everything from us that you requested, perhaps we should end this meeting. It's time for Julianna's feeding."

"Of course." Lizzie got to her feet, accepting she'd ascertained all the information possible from them. "We'll be in touch as soon as we have the DNA results." She led Reena outside.

Behind her, Rolf closed the door a little harder than necessary, as though punctuating the end of the meeting. She hoped for their sake Julianna's DNA didn't match one of the murder victims.

Lizzie replayed the conversation as she headed for her vehicle. Rolf's rude and cagey behavior might be attributed to the fear of losing his daughter. Or had he hidden something, which was why he'd lied about seeking assistance from other adoption agencies?

Based on the short interview, Lizzie had no evidence they were guilty. She understood the heart-wrenching battle many couples faced in trying to adopt. Lizzie hoped they were innocent. However, in the end, none of it mattered if Julianna's DNA confirmed she was one of the stolen babies. Should that happen, Lizzie would be forced to remove her without delay.

She loaded Reena into her SUV and slid into the driver's seat, catching a glimpse of Marina watching her from behind the sheer living room curtain. Lizzie didn't wave, but dread again twisted in her stomach.

Her sweet golden retriever sighed and placed her velvety

nose on Lizzie's forearm. "I knew you'd understand, Reena." She scratched the dog behind her ears, earning her the adoring glance of affection and compassion that only came from a devoted canine. "Too bad you can't detect the legitimacy of the Taylors' adoption."

Reena sighed in agreement and laid her head on the console as Lizzie started the engine. Sometimes her job required tough actions. She pulled away from the house and her thoughts returned to the case.

Lizzie and Reena, along with ten other K-9 officers and their dogs from area police departments, comprised the COK9 unit. Formed by the FBI and funded by Dodger Andrews, the wealthy benefactor of all Colorado K-9 law enforcement programs, the task force was led by an FBI abduction specialist, Supervisory Special Agent Emmett Dane. In the past four months, they'd worked nonstop to find nineteen-year-old Mia Andrews, Dodger's beloved granddaughter. The criminals responsible for kidnapping the pregnant teens, including Mia, believed they'd acquired the perfect victims whom no one would miss. They were wrong. Dodger and COK9's mission was to rescue Mia and bust the illegal adoption ring before anyone else died or other babies were sold on the highly profitable black market. Ideally, they'd reunite the three stolen babies with loving family members.

Lizzie traveled the familiar roads home while thinking about the three victims, teenagers who forensic pathology had confirmed had given birth shortly before their deaths. Initially, their cases weren't connected, and the mothers weren't reported missing because of estrangement from their families and friends. However, the COK9 had ascertained the teens were victims of a killer with a repeating modus operandi. Specifically, manner of death, which consisted of two gunshot wounds to the chest at point-blank range. They were then buried in desolate areas near their Colorado hometowns. The most urgent question was, where were the babies?

Lizzie considered Rolf and Marina. How would this trial affect their marriage? Would their relationship survive if Julianna was removed from their care? Not that Lizzie had any experience in marriage. She'd chosen to remain single since Zeke. One heartbreak per lifetime was more than enough for her.

Her only serious boyfriend, Zeke Doland, had completely buffaloed Lizzie, starting in high school, when their romance began. When the mask came off, he was a complete stranger. Maybe that's what drew Lizzie's heart toward this case. She sympathized with young, vulnerable women.

As usual when memories of Zeke arose, they scrambled with those of his best friend, Walker McCane, who'd cruelly deceived her on their prom night. She'd had a crush on Walker up until then, when he'd betrayed her and Zeke had come to her rescue. She'd stayed with Zeke long-term after that...but he was no knight in shining armor. Just the opposite. Zeke's face bounced to the forefront of her mind, bringing with it the pain of their relationship's demise three years ago—including a murder, a lie and a broken heart.

Having come full circle with her life choices, Lizzie remembered what drew her most to law enforcement. She cared about helping people, and right now, that included babies and a missing pregnant teen.

Lost in her musings and renewed in her mission, Lizzie hadn't realized she'd almost made it home until Reena panted and thudded her tail in recognition. The modest ranch house sat on five acres outside Bison Valley, Colorado, on the eastern side of Denver. Though much of the metropolis had spread and consumed once-remote small towns, Bison Valley remained. Only a half an hour from the big-city chaos, it was close enough to commute when necessary while still giving her the release and freedom of gorgeous scenery. She exhaled at the breathtaking landscape, where the foothills stretched into varying shades of green with pine trees and full bushes, combined with boulders and other rock formations dotting the grounds.

Lizzie's cell rang and she answered with her hands-free Bluetooth device. Dave Cole's contact information lit up her screen. Lizzie worked for the local Bison Valley PD, with Captain Cole as her boss. However, her duty on the task force meant that she also reported to Emmett for the duration of the adoption ring investigation.

"Hey, boss."

"Where are you?" Cole asked.

"Just finished with the Taylor interview for COK9 and pulled into my driveway."

"Sorry to do this to you, but we've got an urgent issue."

"Sir?" Lizzie made a U-turn, returning to the main road. "What happened?"

"A prison transport bus was ambushed. The driver and two corrections officers on board were killed, along with two convicts. Eight others have escaped. It was obviously an orchestrated attack, and there's an APB manhunt in effect," Cole reported. "I texted you the GPS coordinates to the site."

Lizzie's phone chimed with the text. "Got it." She accelerated and closed the kennel divider door, restraining Reena.

"Deputy US marshals are also en route to assist."

An all-hands-on deck kind of response. "Roger that. ETA fifteen minutes." Lizzie disconnected and, using talk-to-text, notified Emmett of the developments and her orders to respond.

From behind her, Reena gave a low growl, then three sharp barks. Lizzie glanced up just as something rammed into the back of her patrol unit. Her vehicle swerved, and she caught the brief flash of a dark SUV in her rearview mirror before a second hit sent her veering to the side. She felt the vehicle skidding off the road until the passenger-side tires slammed hard into the ditch.

Lizzie shifted into Reverse, but her rear tire spun without making contact. She had high centered the vehicle onto something. The road wasn't well traveled, and she was adjacent to the wilderness.

She spotted the dark SUV in her driver's-side mirror. Lizzie braced as the engine roared then the SUV struck again, sending the front end of her vehicle nose-diving into the ditch. With her unit disabled, Lizzie snagged her duty weapon from the console. She watched for the offender to emerge.

Reena whined from inside her kennel. "Down." The dog's nails scuffled, confirming her obedience.

Gunshots pelted off the exterior of Lizzie's patrol unit. She ducked, watching the mirrors. Reena barked and Lizzie hollered, "Reena, down!" The steel dog kennel provided protection from bullets.

Movement to the left caught her attention and she scooted up just enough to peer out and return fire.

Lizzie gripped her radio. "Shots fired, shots fired. Dark SUV, newer model, has me trapped with my K-9. Request backup!" She rattled off the mile marker, monitoring the shooter's vehicle and praying for rescue.

After several rounds, the gunshots finally ceased.

Lizzie froze, not daring to move or breathe. She couldn't hear if the SUV had driven away. When the silence dragged on without incident, she slid upright, staying close to the seat, and peered out the side mirrors. From her vantage point, she couldn't tell if the assailants were still behind her.

The dispatcher chirped that backup was on the way over Lizzie's radio, but she turned down the volume, desperate to listen for the shooter.

Not a sound.

Had he gone?

With her duty weapon in her right hand, Lizzie reached for the handle with her left. She tugged, automatically unlocking it.

The door whipped open and strong hands grabbed her by the

back of her long hair. She glimpsed the masked assailant before he slammed her face into the steering wheel.

Stars danced in front of her eyes and Lizzie lost hold of her gun, which toppled to the floorboard with a thud.

Reena barked wildly from the kennel behind her. Lizzie twisted to reach for her weapon, but the man grabbed her by the calves and jerked her from the seat.

Lizzie kicked, trying to free herself from the assailant's constrictor grip while simultaneously stretching as far as possible to snag her pistol. Her fingernails scraped the black-carpeted floor.

With one last-ditch effort to keep from being yanked out of the vehicle, Lizzie gripped the steering wheel and clung with all her strength. She delivered another hard kick, striking the man with a sickening thud.

The promise of sirens wailed in the distance. *Hang on.*

"Let's go! Cops are coming!" a second man hollered.

Lizzie turned to look just as the assailant slammed the butt of his gun into her temple, sending her into complete darkness.

Deputy US Marshal Walker McCane whipped his unmarked SUV around the corner, speeding ahead of the Bison Valley patrol units. An officer-involved shooting motivated every cop within the sound of the police radio to respond with lights and sirens. Combined with the manhunt for the escaped convicts, law enforcement was already on high alert.

Walker slammed into Park behind the bullet-ridden Bison Valley K-9 SUV and practically leaped out. He rushed to the driver's side, where the officer's legs and black tactical boots hung limply from the open door. A dog's sharp, distressed barks emitted from inside the SUV, and Walker prayed the creature wouldn't attack him as he cautiously approached. Spotting the closed kennel slider, he braced himself for the possible devastating condition of the victim.

The officer lay facedown across the seat and Walker gently repositioned her, then sucked in a startled breath.

It wasn't the crimson streaks that marred her face and nose that sent his heart into arrhythmia—rather the sight of his unconscious high school crush, Lizzie Reynolds. He checked for a pulse, confirming she was alive, and exhaled relief.

She was as beautiful as he recalled, even with the injuries and bruise already developing around her right eye. Like a freight train barreling through his chest, memories of their last encounter slammed into Walker.

It had taken him a full year to work up the courage to ask Lizzie to their senior prom. His excitement at her acceptance tanked when she'd left the dance with his ex–best friend, Zeke Doland. Her painful and public rejection had added to the gaping heart wounds his mother's abandonment had created in him as a child. The recollection ignited a fire inside Walker. Two betrayals in one night.

Lizzie groaned, returning his attention to her. The sounds of other responding units squealing onto the scene registered somewhere in the back of his mind, but his complete focus remained on Lizzie.

He shoved away the unbidden thoughts. The past didn't matter right now. All those offenses had happened more than a decade ago. *Get over it, McCane.* Yet the reasoning did nothing to diminish the sting.

Walker had worked too hard to get where he was, and he'd not stumble over his own discarded emotions. His job was his top and only priority. He had to go on a moment's notice when dispatched around the state. He didn't have time for a personal life outside his career. His ex-girlfriend, JoLynn, hadn't understood the marshal world. They hadn't been a good match for many reasons, but none of that mattered other than to solidify his resolve to focus on his career.

"Step away from the vehicle with your hands up," a man hollered from behind Walker.

The realization that the officer probably thought Walker was trying to hurt Lizzie had Walker raising his hands in surrender. "I'm Deputy US Marshal Walker McCane. My badge is clipped to my hip." He shifted ever so slightly to reveal his credentials. "Officer Lizzie Reynolds is injured inside the vehicle."

"Take two steps backward, keeping your hands where I can see them," the officer ordered, ignoring Walker's comment.

Walker did as instructed, and the officer rushed behind him. Once he'd patted down Walker, simultaneously spotting and confirming his credentials, he holstered his gun. "Procedure," he explained.

"I understand. I need to check on her." Walker returned to Lizzie, not waiting for his approval. "Hey, Lizzie, are you okay?"

She groaned again, slowly coming to. Her long eyelashes fluttered, and she opened her eyes, staring past him. She placed a finger against her nose and winced.

Walker spotted a small tissue box in her door panel and withdrew a few, passing them to her. She took the offering and dabbed at the injuries.

"Thanks," she rasped through a stuffy nose.

He helped Lizzie sit up and stepped from the confined space, allowing the Bison Valley officer to speak with her. He stayed close, awkwardly rehearsing his next words.

After she'd assured them she was fine, Lizzie slid out of the vehicle, then leaned against the side panel.

A second officer, who Walker now realized was Captain Cole, based on his collar brass and the name plate on his uniform, helped to steady her. "Lizzie, are you sure you're all right? I'll call for an ambulance."

She waved him off. "I'm fine. Let me release Reena. She's scared." Lizzie opened the rear driver's-side door and a large golden retriever bounded out, sniffing, her tail wagging. "I'm okay," she assured the K-9, stroking her golden fur.

Lizzie explained how an SUV had pulled up behind her and begun shooting. "If the attackers—there were at least two," she clarified, "hadn't heard the responding units' sirens, I don't know what would've happened."

"Did they say anything?" Captain Cole asked.

"The one who attacked me never spoke, but his partner warned they had to leave before you all arrived." Lizzie's attention shifted to Walker, and she blinked several times as though registering his presence for the first time. "Walker McCane, what are you doing here?" Evidently, she wasn't fully cognizant of her surroundings if it took her that long to recognize him. In all fairness, he was equally surprised to see her.

"Here to assist with the manhunt for the escaped convicts," he said.

"Bison Valley Captain Dave Cole." The uniformed man extended a hand in Walker's direction, which he quickly reciprocated. "We appreciate the extra help."

"A prisoner escaping is a pretty big deal in the marshal world," Walker replied. "Another DUSM will join me as soon as possible."

"Escaped convicts are not something we want Bison Valley known for," Cole grumbled.

"I'm only aware of what I overheard on the callout," Walker said. "Any updated information?"

"Negative. We're still trying to positively identify the prisoners, guards and driver," Cole said. "The extensive damage to the bus is delaying the process."

"The two men who attacked me couldn't have obtained a vehicle that fast," Lizzie replied.

"Never underestimate the creativity and ingenuity of desperate criminals," Walker said dryly. "They might've carjacked someone on the road."

"I hadn't considered that," Lizzie agreed.

"Based on the orchestrated ambush, it appears they had sufficient ammunition at their disposal," Cole added. "Deputy Marshal McCane, Lizzie is a great resource, as she grew up here. Since you already know each other, I'd suggest the two of you combine efforts."

Walker stiffened. Not what he wanted to hear.

"Not necessary," Lizzie replied. "Walker and I went to high school together. He's also familiar with the area."

"Even better reason for you to partner." Cole's gaze bounced from Walker to Lizzie. "Two locals means we don't have to get you caught up on the landscape. Lizzie and her brilliant K-9 are my best tracking team. We need those fugitives caught fast before they unleash havoc on our town. You three will be a force to be reckoned with."

"Are you sure you're okay to proceed?" Walker asked.

Lizzie's lip flattened into a thin line. "I'm fine."

"Once we've documented this scene, let's rally at the command post. I'll send you the location via text. I've got the list of escapees there and we can work on our game plan." Cole headed for the second officer, already capturing pictures of Lizzie's vehicle. He collected the bullet casings into evidence bags and labeled them.

"Introduce me to your partner." Walker gestured at the retriever.

"This is Reena."

"May I?"

"Absolutely."

Walker knelt and offered his hand, allowing Reena to sniff her approval before he petted the dog. "Hopefully you can find these prisoners before they do any more damage." He rose and faced Lizzie. "Any idea why someone would come after you?"

"I'm not exactly making friends with criminals in my current role," she quipped.

"I don't imagine so." Walker smiled, remembering her quick wit.

"I'm finished here," the officer said and walked back to his vehicle without waiting for their response.

"Follow me and I'll lead you to the command post," Lizzie said to Walker, not introducing them.

Walker nodded and slid behind the wheel of his SUV, contemplating the astronomical odds of collaborating on a prison break manhunt with Lizzie after ten years.

He trailed her patrol unit to a cordoned-off campground outside of town where local, state and federal law enforcement had combined their efforts and were working from a mobile command post. The large, unmarked black motor home sat adjacent to the parking area, and patrol vehicles consumed every available space.

He joined her and they entered the command post together. Several people worked at desks while the computer monitors mounted on two of the walls displayed news reports of the situation. Radio chatter filled the atmosphere, mingling with conversations between those bustling in and out of the confined space. Captain Cole stood at the far side holding a phone to his ear. He held up a finger, indicating they needed to wait.

Lizzie moved to where a whiteboard revealed the manifest names of those involved in the ambush. A large, detailed map with red lines and circled areas hung beside it. Walker approached, studying both. Ten prisoners', two corrections officers' and the bus driver's names were listed along with their status. Most were blank except the driver and guards who were marked *presumed DOA*, the acronym for dead on arrival.

Reena stayed close to Lizzie, flicking Walker an occasional curious glance. Lizzie placed her fingertip at the edge of the name Eddie Waterhouse. "That name is familiar."

"How so?" Walker asked.

"He was involved in a robbery and shooting when I worked for Littleton PD."

"That's one person with motive to come after you, right?" Walker asked.

"It's possible, but why now after three years?"

Walker didn't reply. There was no statute of limitations on revenge where criminals were connected.

Captain Cole advanced, still holding the phone against his ear. "Thanks for the update," he said, disconnecting and dropping his cell into his pocket. "We've got updated information on two of the convicts." He took a dry-erase marker and wrote *deceased* beside Eddie Waterhouse and Neal Caywood. "The crime scene technicians are verifying identities based on the prisoners' identity bracelets. However, some have significant injuries, so we'll have to wait until the medical examiner makes that determination." He shook his head. "Shame the guards and driver were also killed."

"Waterhouse was the only lead we had so far." Walker hesitated then moved closer. "Wait." He spotted the name Gregory Juhl. "Juhl was a fugitive we recovered about six years ago."

"That doesn't explain him targeting Lizzie," Cole said.

"True."

"Maybe they're unrelated," Lizzie replied. "We don't know that my assailants are the escaped convicts."

"I'd argue the attack wasn't random," Walker said. "Not way out there."

Lizzie frowned. "Right."

Captain Cole traced the highlighted route. "The bus was traveling south from the correctional facility in Sterling to Cañon City. The ambush occurred close to the foothills."

"Giving the escapees plenty of wilderness to hide themselves," Walker surmised.

"Where do you want us to start?" Lizzie asked.

Cole pointed to the map. "Teams are working a grid here. I'd like you and Deputy Marshal McCane to move toward Raspberry Butte, so you'll be covering fresh ground while keeping in line with them."

"Copy that." Walker snapped a picture of the map with his cell phone.

"Don't you need to wait for your partner?" Lizzie's gaze flicked between Captain Cole and Walker.

Did she not want to work with him? Walker bristled. He had no desire to hang out with Lizzie, either, even if he was curious about how she worked with her canine companion. He didn't care to revisit their history. Though, based on the way she made his palms sweat, she still affected his senses.

No way. Romance had no place in his life, especially after witnessing his parents' divorce. His father and Walker maintained a close relationship after his mother's abandonment. And that's the way Walker liked it. Simple and uncomplicated. His work kept him busy and on the road.

He and Lizzie would maintain a professional relationship and find the fugitives. Nothing more. At least it appeared the feeling was mutual. He forced neutrality into his tone. "I'll send him the information, and he can join us."

"Perfect." Cole handed Lizzie a plastic bag with fabric inside just as his cell phone rang again. "Supplies are near the door. Excuse me." He stepped away, answering the call.

Walker gestured at the bag.

"They're scent articles collected from the prison bus for Reena to work with," Lizzie explained.

"Gotcha." Walker started toward his unit. "I need to grab my gear."

"Same." Lizzie and Reena moved to hers.

Once they'd donned backpacks, they dropped in the supplies, which included water, small yellow flags and granola bars, along with matches and a nonflammable flare gun for emergencies. Lastly, they clipped radios onto their belts.

"Guess we'd better head out." Lizzie's tone held the enthusiasm of a zombie. She opened the scent article bag and offered the items to Reena.

Intrigued at the team's process, Walker watched as the K-9 sniffed the fabric. "How does she know which person we're tracking?"

"She's cataloging the scents like individual pieces of paper," Lizzie said. "Each is unique to her."

"Interesting."

They hiked from the command post toward Raspberry Butte. The ground quickly shifted into a steep incline.

"They at least picked a gorgeous location to disappear." Walker attempted to alleviate the awkward moment.

Lizzie and Reena took the lead when the trail narrowed, permitting one hiker at a time. "And a place where finding them will be nothing short of a needle in the proverbial mountain haystack."

"Will Reena be able to follow their scent?" Walker asked, trying to maintain conversation.

"If they're out here, yes, without a doubt."

Far be it from Walker to argue with her. He'd tracked fugitives, but not through the mountains. The terrain was rough, uneven and rocky. On the reverse side, the thick forest shadowed them from the hot summer sun.

They'd trekked for about twenty minutes before Lizzie said, "Depending on how familiar our fugitives are with the terrain, I doubt they'll go off the trails."

"Their desperation to escape will motivate them," Walker disputed.

"That could also be true."

The dry earth concealed footprint depressions, making tracing them difficult. Still, they continued searching, taking only short breaks.

Two hours later, Lizzie paused. "Let's take ten," she said, perching on a massive boulder. Reena panted beside her.

"Is she okay?" Walker withdrew his bottled water and swiped at his forehead.

"Yeah, thankfully the trees are keeping the August temperature bearable for her." Lizzie took a swig and poured the rest into a portable bowl for the golden retriever.

The silence between them lasted uncomfortably longer than Walker preferred until he suggested they proceed. Their trail took them higher through the mountains, the air thinning with each step. The enormous boulders and thick forest provided far too many hiding places for the escapees.

By the time the sun had started to set without any leads, the overall frustration between them was palpable. The scent of rain filled the atmosphere. Clouds roiled overhead with the deep rumble of thunder and the promise of a storm. In perfect tandem, the commander radioed, ordering the searchers to return to the BOO, referencing the base of operations, ASAP, as an immense thunderstorm was predicted to hit the area. He assured they'd resume the hunt first thing in the morning.

"Great, that gives the fugitives more time to disappear," Walker grumbled.

Lizzie didn't respond.

They returned to the command post, marking their search areas on the map and exiting with the group of disgruntled officers. Walker's cell phone pinged with a text message from Kelan Evans, his partner deputy US marshal. Got hung up in court today. Be there ASAP.

Walker responded, No worries. Manhunt called off for weather. Will resume at first light.

Reconsidering the travel time from Denver to Raspberry Butte, Walker stopped to talk with Captain Cole. "Sir, do you recommend any lodging nearby?"

Cole shook his head. "Unless you can find someone willing to split a room with you, doubtful. Most of the volunteers have already booked with the local places." Then Cole snapped his fingers. "Hey, Lizzie, don't you still have that garage apartment for rent?"

Lizzie gaped in displeasure at her boss's suggestion.

"Not a problem." Walker frowned, kicking himself for not thinking ahead. Especially in a rural area with few options. "My partner will also need lodging, too, anyway."

Lizzie's forced smile didn't reach her eyes. "Captain Cole is correct. You and your partner are welcome to stay in the vacant apartment over the garage. I've been trying to lease it and haven't had much interest. It's very basic, but there's a bathroom and beds for two people." She shrugged. "No pressure, though. It's nothing fancy."

"Thanks, Lizzie, that'll expedite you getting started tomorrow." Cole didn't wait for a reply but turned his attention to another officer.

Fantastic. Walker inwardly cringed while his brain argued the ramifications. He'd not intended to be alone with Lizzie, which might result in facing their past. Not something he was prepared to deal with. Best-case scenario, she'd avoid it as much as him. But bunking at her house meant he wouldn't have to make the long commute early in the morning. He and Kelan wouldn't be in the same house as her, he reasoned. And it was only for a night.

On another note, Walker considered that someone had intentionally attempted to hurt Lizzie. The protective instincts that benefited him in his job rose to the surface, overriding the relationship insecurities that had plagued him since his teenage years. This wasn't about them, it was about catching a group of escaped convicts. What would it hurt to stick close to her for one night? Except, he had to ask the question troubling him. It meant dredging up the past, but it was unavoidable and her response might change everything. "Will Zeke mind us crashing there?"

"Not an issue." Lizzie averted her eyes and didn't elaborate, leaving Walker with more questions than answers.

TWO

Walker's question took Lizzie aback. To avoid a Zeke-sized conversation with him, she said, "If you're uncomfortable with the arrangement—"

"No, not at all. I appreciate the offer. Thank you." His blue eyes seemed to challenge her.

"Great." Lizzie forced another smile. "Follow me. I live outside of Bison Valley." She turned without giving him a chance to respond.

She loaded Reena into the SUV and slid behind the wheel as a spattering of rain flicked the windshield. What random act of bizarre had brought Walker McCane back into her life? And why now? And why did he have to look so good? If he was ugly, she'd have a much better chance of ignoring him, but there was nothing unattractive about Walker. He'd grown into a drop-dead gorgeous guy.

Lizzie groaned. His handsome exterior didn't eliminate their past. And the last thing she needed was to lose focus when they had a handful of escaped convicts to track down. At least his partner would also be staying at the apartment. The third party ensured she and Walker wouldn't delve into personal conversations.

By the time they'd reached the highway, the skies parted, and a deluge immersed the area, making it hard to see a foot in front of her. She left the kennel divider open, allowing Reena to stay close. "This is not how I planned for today to go," she grumbled to her companion. As if trekking through the wilderness with Walker wasn't bad enough, he'd be a temporary guest in her garage apartment. "Ugh."

Reena nudged her arm, and Lizzie offered a quick scratch behind her soft ears.

"Sorry, girl, gotta keep both hands on the wheel in this storm," she apologized, withdrawing her touch. Reena sighed understanding.

With her windshield wipers swishing wildly, she slowed to allow for the treacherous conditions. Walker's headlights beamed in her rearview mirror, confirming he'd done the same.

Lizzie turned onto the gravel lane that led to her simple ranch, and a slash of lightning briefly illuminated the property. She pressed the garage remote, and the large door opened. Lizzie pulled in and Walker parked behind her. She stepped out of her unit just as Walker ducked into the garage, soaked from the downpour.

"You can access the apartment from the side steps, but I need to get the key and supplies. Follow me inside." Lizzie released Reena, then headed for the side door, Walker trailing with his duffel bag.

Had she tidied up the house before she left? She shrugged off the worry. She wasn't impressing Walker, just providing him a place to crash for the night.

"Shut the door," Lizzie ordered once they'd crossed the threshold.

Walker did as she instructed, and she flicked on the living room lamp, illuminating the spacious room. Her overstuffed sofa and recliner appeared lonely, no doubt created for a large family.

Another sliver of light split the sky, revealing the forest adjacent to the house through the picture window. For the first time since owning the property, a twinge of fear oozed through Lizzie. She wrapped her arms around herself, fending off the images of the masked man who'd tried to force her from the SUV.

"Are you all right?" Walker's question jerked her to the present.

"I'll grab a towel for you and Reena to dry off," Lizzie replied, ignoring his question. Then, to her dog, she ordered, "Reena, stay." She sat beside Walker, offering him a curious glance. "Be right back." Lizzie hurried to snag the linens, then returned, first passing one to Walker before she started drying Reena's long fur. She gathered extra bedding and towels and returned to where Walker still waited beside Reena. "The key is hanging by the door."

Walker turned and snagged the brass key.

"The apartment is furnished, but you'll need these." She held the items tighter, leading him into the garage again. "This should be fun," she grumbled, then darted into the rain.

They jogged up the steps leading to the garage apartment, and Walker quickly inserted the key. They scooted inside and shut the door. Lizzie set the linens on the dining table and flicked on the overhead light, illuminating the room. A kitchenette with a two-person table and a sofa/sleeper consumed the space.

"There's one bedroom, a bathroom with a shower, and that—" she pointed to the sofa "—converts to a queen-size bed."

"Thank you again for allowing Kelan and me to stay," Walker replied.

"It's not much." Lizzie shrugged.

"This is great." He set his bag on the floor and faced her. "See ya tomorrow." Lizzie started for the door. "Unless—"

Lizzie faced him. "What?"

"I wouldn't mind going over the case a little."

The sky lit up again with a flash of lightning. "Sure. I took a picture of the command-post board," Lizzie offered, surprising herself. "We could see if we find anything to help with the manhunt."

"Works for me."

They returned to her house and strode to the kitchen. "I need to update my supervisor, Emmett," she said, withdrawing her phone and typing a text to the task force leader. He responded affirmatively.

"Good?" Walker asked.

"Yep." Lizzie tucked her cell into her pocket. "How about something warm to drink?" She lifted a pack of instant hot cocoa from the cabinet.

"Only if you have whipped cream to top it."

"Is there any other way to drink it?"

Walker grinned. "Not in my book." While she prepared the steaming mugs, he studied the picture of the command board on her phone.

She slid a notepad and pen to him. "You looked like you needed this."

"You read my mind." He scribbled the escapees' names. "Captain Cole has most likely already created a list of likely places, relatives and acquaintances where the prisoners might go for help, but I'm not assuming anything."

"Right, better to have a plan. If nothing else, we can merge information." Lizzie slid a steaming mug over to him and topped it off with canned whipped cream, then did the same for hers. "Rainy days transform me into a kid again." As soon as the words escaped her lips, Lizzie longed to retract them. The last thing she wanted was to remind Walker of their younger years.

He sipped. "I haven't had hot cocoa in ages."

"It seemed appropriate with the storm."

"Good call." Walker seemed to study her before quickly averting his eyes.

Was he remembering their prom night, too, when she'd caught him kissing Presley Quintana? She'd been devastated and Zeke had rushed to console her, then offered to drive her home.

The memory stung, even now. Zeke said Walker had only asked Lizzie to prom to make Presley jealous. It made sense to Lizzie, since she hadn't been popular, just a book nerd with a huge crush on a guy completely out of her league. Had he known she liked him? She wanted to ask, but what benefit was there in dredging up the past?

She blamed herself. Lizzie had dreamed of being that wallflower in the cheesy teen movies who becomes a princess, swept off her feet by the hero. Instead, she'd had the rug ripped out from beneath her. Zeke had come to her rescue, a knight in a white tuxedo, caring, kind and supportive. That was the start of their relationship, and she'd thought it was fate. Until the horrible night of the shooting three years ago that forever changed the trajectory of her career and her life.

Lizzie studied Walker, comparing the high school version she'd known a decade ago—gangly, shy and awkward—to this handsome, confident, muscular man sitting at her counter. Was he thinking about Zeke and blaming her for the demise of their friendship? Their proximity was bad enough, as they both avoided discussing their history and what constituted the worst prom night ever.

Zeke had claimed he wanted to warn Lizzie about Walker, but he'd feared losing his best friend. Later he blamed her for getting between them. Zeke had said and done all the right things until his true colors emerged, and over time he'd transformed into a man she abhorred. His propensity to lie had finally betrayed him. And she felt like a fool for believing him.

They'd dated seriously, then both joined the Littleton Police Department. Images of the liquor store robbery and the shooting—the incident involving the recently deceased Eddie Waterhouse—returned. Zeke had lied in defending his actions to their commander—and anyone else who'd listen—regarding Jennifer Mace's death. But Lizzie had seen the truth and reported it to their boss.

She shook off the intrusive thoughts. That was irrelevant right now, and it was unnecessary to rehash the past with Walker. She especially wouldn't share how Zeke's illegal actions in Jennifer's death had snowballed into her resignation from the LPD. But not before had Zeke begged her to cover for him. She'd weighed the cost and refused. It hadn't mattered because, her life had still fallen apart as a result. She'd lost her boyfriend, her reputation and her job. The whole situation had made her look idiotic.

Walker glanced up, catching her. Lizzie's face warmed with embarrassment, but his next words threw her off completely. "I must ask again. Are you sure Zeke wouldn't mind me being here?"

She blinked several times, searching her brain for an elusive response that would satisfy Walker. Her failed relationship with Zeke was one topic she refused to discuss. Especially with Walker. "It's a nonissue because we're not together anymore. I live alone." Why had she added the last part? Lizzie didn't elaborate further, and thankfully, Walker didn't press. It wasn't untruthful, but the reminders had her reasserting that she and Walker weren't friends—they were coworkers on this case and nothing more. They'd go their separate ways once they apprehended the escaped convicts. None of this investigation required rehashing old wounds.

An awkward silence hovered between them, and Lizzie regretted the cocoa offer. She should've gone to bed. Now she'd have to make an excuse to leave the room.

"Are you okay?" Walker asked.

"Just tired and have a lot on my mind." Not a lie.

"I've been brainstorming why someone came after you tonight. Any ideas?"

Grateful for the shift in topics, Lizzie shook her head. "Eddie's is the only name of the escaped convicts that I recognized. And since he died in the ambush, that leaves no one."

"Perhaps whoever attacked you wanted to steal your car. You were in a remote area, and we have eight missing prisoners."

"Maybe." Lizzie wasn't convinced that was the motive, though she couldn't explain why. Her cell phone rang and Captain Cole's name appeared on the screen. "Give me a second." She answered the call, turning her back to Walker. "We made it safely to my place."

"Good. The storm has picked up momentum."

As though emphasizing his assessment, a gust of wind whipped rain against the windows.

"But that's not why I'm calling. Please put me on speakerphone with Deputy Marshal McCane."

Lizzie did as he asked. "Go ahead."

"The evidence techs found a piece of paper with an annotated list of names," Cole began. "The finding drastically changes this manhunt."

Walker's right eyebrow peaked, reminding Lizzie of the man's younger self.

"Who's on the list?" Walker asked.

"Bill McCane, Walker McCane, Lizzie Reynolds."

Lizzie sucked in a breath, her gaze locked with Walker's. "Why us?"

"And my father?" Walker inserted.

"That's our conundrum," Cole said. "Effective immediately, all three of you are ordered into protective custody."

"Negative," Walker and Lizzie replied in unison.

"I'll move my dad to a safe house, but I'm working this case," Walker said. "However, I agree that after what happened to Lizzie on the road, she should go into WitSec."

Lizzie bristled at the comment. "No way. I'm not playing a disgusting game of hide-and-seek from deranged criminals. Besides, if they're after us, there's a reason. It's critical for us to figure that out—cooperatively."

"She makes a valid point," Walker said.

Lizzie shot him an appreciative glance.

"I assumed you'd say that," Cole said. "Let's start with why you'd be on this list."

"Unsure," Lizzie replied. "We're searching for connections with the list of convicts."

"Keep me updated."

They disconnected, and Walker rose. "I need to make a few calls."

Lizzie gave him privacy and moved the portable whiteboard from her home office to the dining room table. She wrote the escapees' names and added the names of the deceased guards and driver. Then she booted up her laptop to research.

Walker joined her with his computer. "My partner, Kelan Evans, was supposed to join us in the manhunt, but he got caught up in court and another case. He's handling the transport and security for my father and will be here ASAP."

"I'm glad you have someone you trust to do that. But I'd totally understand if you had to leave."

"Not happening. Whoever took the time to write out our names is serious about getting to us. Let's find out why, and quickly. The longer the escapees have to trudge through the mountains, the less chance we have of finding them."

"True." Lizzie considered the note. "Who do we have in common?"

Walker crossed his arms over his chest, brows furrowed. "Not a clue."

"Me, either." Lizzie tapped the capped marker on the table. "And without knowledge of their wilderness survival skills, for all we know the escapees could be deep into the woods by now."

"Someone helping the convicts from the outside would explain the orchestrated ambush." Walker studied the names. "The positive side is we know to be extra vigilant."

"Ugh, it also adds credence that my attack wasn't random." Lizzie involuntarily shivered at the thought of escaped prisoners holding a female cop hostage and the depravity of what they'd do to her. She reconsidered the names of the escaped convicts. "You mentioned you'd arrested Gregory Juhl. What else can you tell me about him?"

"He was convicted of illegal narcotics possession and distribution. He escaped custody but didn't get far. He's not that bright, but he probably has connections on the outside." Walker pointed to the next name. "Kelan reminded me he arrested Anthony Arnold a while back as well. Arnold's also a known drug dealer. Not a vast reach to think Juhl and Arnold bonded over their mutual crime link."

Lizzie made notes on the board, drawing a dotted line between Juhl and Arnold. "Good, that's a start. Revenge is a common motive and gives credence to why they're coming after you and your dad." Lizzie crossed her arms and leaned against the wall. "Except that doesn't explain them targeting me."

"Please reconsider protective custody," Walker said again. "Whoever's pursuing you wants you alive. If they'd intended to kill you—"

"Um, they shot at me, so don't jump to that conclusion." Even as she said the words, Lizzie realized the error in her thinking. Anyone who'd planned to finish her off might've relished the opportunity after extracting her from her patrol unit. "Disregard. On the bright side, they might keep coming." She quipped, "I'll lure them out from under their hiding rocks."

"Nope. There's no way I'm letting you serve yourself up as bait."

"Let me?" Lizzie skewered him with a glare. "May I kindly remind you I'm a trained police officer, capable of protecting and defending myself?"

Walker lifted hands in surrender. "I didn't mean to offend you."

"For the record, I'm not playing with fire for an ego boost here. I'm investigating another case for the COK9 team, and I can't do that without doing the work."

Walker tilted his head. "I'm intrigued. Tell me more."

Why had she mentioned the task force? "The FBI pulled the group together, with the mission of identifying and taking down an illegal adoption ring. Their MO is to abduct and murder expecting teenage mothers, then steal and sell their babies."

"That's unconscionable." Walker shook his head, disgust written in his expression.

"That's why we're going on the offensive." Lizzie faced the board again. "So, what do you know about Arnold and Juhl on a personal level?"

"Unless something major has changed, neither had a girlfriend or family member willing to cooperate with law enforcement."

"Let's make some calls, anyway. LKAs."

Walker withdrew his laptop from his backpack and, after several keyboard sounds, provided Lizzie with Anthony Arnold's last known address and contact information while he called about Gregory Juhl. Within a few minutes, they'd reached another dead end.

"This is beyond frustrating," Walker said.

Lizzie walked to the kitchen and returned with two bottles of water. "If revenge is the mission for them targeting you and your dad, is it because you tossed Juhl back into jail after he escaped custody six years ago?"

"It's possible. Arnold wouldn't come after me unless he's getting paid for it." Walker's eyebrows peaked. "Wait. Maybe that's it. Whoever orchestrated the ambush—and I'm guessing it wasn't the prisoners—might be the same person ordering the hit on us."

"Hired killers aren't concerned with correlation. They'd provide a shopping list of people they wanted dead." Lizzie made a note on the board, adding to the possible motives.

"If that's the case, they'll continue coming after us, and we may never figure out if it's the convicts or whoever paid them."

"We need to be on constant red alert."

"Agreed. And I appreciate you allowing Kelan and me to crash in the apartment." Walker grinned. "Although you might regret it, because now you're stuck with us until we resolve this."

Lizzie opened her mouth to protest, then changed her mind. "Why have a guest apartment if not for marshal cooperation?" she deadpanned. Her cell phone buzzed with a text from Captain

Cole. Without explaining, she walked to the living room window and peered out the corner of the curtains. A Bison Valley PD patrol unit sat parked outside. "Cole texted that he's ordered an officer to conduct perimeter watch."

"Good. We'll take all the help we can get."

Lizzie glanced at the clock. "I either need to go to bed or eat. Are you hungry?" Needing a little distance to gather her emotions and focus on the task at hand, Lizzie moved to the kitchen.

"Always," Walker teased. "And I prefer to sleep on a full stomach, anyway."

She chuckled and opened the freezer. "I've got a couple of frozen pizzas."

"Perfect. Reminds me of high school. Zeke and I devoured four at a sitting. My dad got so mad. He'd say, 'I just went to the store. That was supposed to last weeks.' And I was clueless."

"Teenage hunger and metabolism," Lizzie replied, ignoring the Zeke comment.

"Yeah." Walker sat at the dining table.

"How is your father?"

"He's doing well. Retired and getting used to his free time. Which means he calls me. A lot." Walker grimaced good-naturedly.

Lizzie busied herself preparing the pizzas, feeling a little envious. Her family didn't communicate often if ever. They went about their own lives, apart from one another. She slid into a chair opposite him. The same butterflies that once flitted in her stomach when she was around Walker returned. As though no time had passed, and the painful prom incident had never occurred. Or her emotions had a lousy memory, since the nervousness hadn't lessened.

Walker had grown into a competent man whose presence and badge demanded respect. Lizzie's emotions plunged her into the gawkiness of a crushing teenager. Ugh. She had to view him in a different light, or this would be a seriously long case. *Pretend he's mean and ugly.*

"High school seems like a hundred years ago," Walker interrupted her thoughts.

Lizzie held her breath. She did not want to mention that or Zeke or anything related to before and after. To her relief, Walker steered the topics around classes they had together and their favorite teachers. The easy conversation allowed her to relax.

Zeke had taught her a romantic relationship with another law enforcement officer complicated her life and distracted her from doing her job to the fullest. Especially where career competition ruled as king. She studied Walker, wondering if he was involved with anyone. If he was, he'd not revealed it, and she'd not ask. Did he think of her? *Knock it off, Lizzie.* It didn't matter. He'd betrayed her once, and although they'd been young, it didn't excuse the behavior, nor would she permit him to hurt her again.

Walker laughed and Lizzie caught herself, realizing she'd daydreamed and totally missed the conversation.

"Heard you left Colorado after high school," she said. "Why'd you return?" Now, why bring that up? Seriously, she needed to go to bed.

Based on Walker's expression, she instantly realized her mistake.

Walker contemplated Lizzie's question. Had she kept tabs on his whereabouts—or, in his case, his cowardly fleeing from the state? If so, why? She'd mentioned that she and Zeke were no longer a couple. Where had his backstabbing friend gone?

"Long story," Walker replied, determined not to divulge anything more than necessary. He'd not admit his insecurities to her. Ever. Instead, he focused on the fond memories of Nick Lancaster that came to mind. A slam of grief unexpectedly hit him, remembering the mentor he'd lost to cancer.

"You don't have to—" Lizzie said.

"No. It's okay." Walker sorted his thoughts, then said, "After finishing my criminal justice degree in Nebraska, I joined Omaha PD. Met a state marshal at an event. We connected, and he mentored me, later convincing me to apply. I got on with the marshals and never looked back." He didn't add he'd not considered DUSM as a career path before Nick. The man had influenced Walker's faith and confidence.

"How long have you been with them?" Lizzie asked.

"Four years. He transferred me to Colorado, so I was grateful for that." He omitted that leaving Colorado had given him a fresh start from the pain of losing his best friend and his high school crush.

"I've been with Bison Valley that same amount of time."

"I assumed you'd worked for them longer than that."

Lizzie averted her eyes.

What had he said wrong?

"Um, right after the academy I got hired with Littleton PD. I later returned to Bison Valley, and Captain Cole started me as a canine handler." He didn't miss the way she quickly shifted topics. "Reena's amazing to work with." At the mention of her name, the golden retriever moseyed over to them and placed her head in Lizzie's lap. She ran her fingers through the dog's fur, eliciting a wag of approval.

"She's a sweet girl." Walker extended his hand. Reena moved closer, allowing him to pet her. "Zeke always talked about being a cop." He dropped the subject like a flashbang and waited for the explosion. Just as he expected, it was the blast from a siren that sucked the oxygen from the room. *Okay, time to deal with this monster.* "Hey, we danced around him most of the night."

She groaned. "Fair enough."

"Did you make the career jump together?"

"Yes." Lizzie exhaled a long breath, and Reena took the cue, returning to her bed in the living room.

Walker admired the way the team communicated without words.

"Zeke convinced me to enter the police academy with him, and at first, it was a lot of fun. Then it became clear the competitiveness enthralled him. He always had to score higher than me, and if I beat him, he'd pout until the next exam." She rolled her eyes. "It got old fast. But I guess that's my fault for thinking men will work with women without feeling intimidated."

"I have several female colleagues. I value their work ethic and contribution."

"Good to know."

"What happened with Zeke?" Walker asked.

"Things just didn't work out."

For the first time, Walker spotted the sadness that lingered in Lizzie's eyes. He longed to know about her life since high school. The thought of facing his ex–best friend roused his own competitiveness. He wasn't the quiet teen sidekick he'd once been. Thanks to the mentorship and his years of law enforcement experience, he'd developed the confidence and muscles he needed to excel. "I'm sorry to hear that." Was he?

"All in the past. Anyway, I learned not to date a guy in the same profession. Once burned, twice shy." Though she said the words lightly, disappointment unexpectedly careened into Walker.

"Relationships and my job are a bad combination. I don't have the time to dedicate to another person." The comment was true, but as soon as he spoke the words, Walker realized he'd opened the door for Lizzie to ask questions. And he wasn't rehashing his failed love life. His work was his top priority and getting over Lizzie had made him Mr. Noncommittal, as JoLynn had nicknamed him. She wasn't wrong. But Walker's heart was guarded under lock and key, and he had zero plans of changing that.

Part of him was thrilled Zeke was out of the picture, but there was no mistaking her comment, and he soaked it in. No, he shoved aside the thoughts, appeasing his mind that with the established boundary, she'd not get the wrong idea about their cooperative efforts. But his heart contended the rationalization. Not that he planned to ask her out. They'd finally established peace in their relationship.

"I didn't answer your earlier question, though. I went into law enforcement because I connected with vulnerable teen girls who were like me at that age—naive and needing protection," Lizzie replied, clearly done discussing relationship issues. She also didn't elaborate. "I guess it's why this COK9 case means so much to me."

He appreciated that. "I get it." And he really did. If he could talk to eighteen-year-old Walker, he'd tell him to ditch Zeke and focus on Lizzie. *What? Where did that come from?* He cleared his throat. "Kids need guidance."

"If I'd known better, I might've avoided a lot of pain." Her gaze drilled through him, and he swallowed hard.

Did she mean him? Surely not. Evidently, Zeke had done a number on her. Fury that his ex–best friend had dared to hurt Lizzie confused Walker. It wasn't his business. And yet, he cared. She'd done great things with her life, and he was impressed, almost proud of her, but Zeke's name put him on edge.

Should he mention prom? Surely by now, Zeke had told her the truth. Even if he hadn't, Walker wouldn't badmouth an ex-boyfriend to gain a woman's affection. Basically, he wasn't Zeke.

As a kid, Walker had seen Zeke as fun and adventurous, but hindsight and maturity revealed Zeke was rebellious, deceitful and a troublemaker. How they'd both avoided juvenile detention was a surprise to Walker.

Whenever Zeke had gotten caught for his antics, he'd blamed Walker as it benefited him. Thankfully, no one seemed to believe Zeke. But it had taken Walker a long time to see through his lying friend. Maybe he and Lizzie had that in common. Though he'd not vandalized school property or stolen from the local convenience store like Zeke, Walker hadn't separated himself from the jerk. As Nick had taught him, compliance was acceptance. The final straw was Zeke coercing and paying Presley Quintana to kiss Walker in front of Lizzie at the prom. The move had stunned Walker into silence, and he'd never forgotten the pain in Lizzie's eyes as she'd turned and ran away. His ex–best friend had put him through enough, and he couldn't imagine what he'd done to Lizzie.

Knowing Lizzie and Zeke had become a couple after that night had devastated Walker. He'd consoled himself that she was happy. Besides, he wasn't relationship material. Lizzie had always been classier than him. His horribly painful shyness had plagued him and left him dateless for most of his life, aside from the relationship with JoLynn, which fizzled out when his job took precedence. He'd focused on work and faith, trusting the combination to protect his heart.

"Hey, something occurred to me. I don't recall you mentioning your mom. Do you think she's in danger, too?" Lizzie asked.

Walker glanced down. "Doubtful. She left when I was in high school. Haven't heard from or seen her since." He wouldn't tell her how his mother's abandonment had completely changed Walker's personality. He'd never shared that with anyone except Zeke, who'd used the secret to torment Walker with degrading and hurtful comments about how nobody loved him, including his mom. Zeke had intended to isolate Walker into believing his friend was the only one trustworthy. Now Walker identified the manipulation technique, and it caused his blood to boil.

"Oh. I'm sorry."

Walker had stupidly assumed Zeke was also his biggest ally. Until he'd swept Lizzie away. He'd confronted Zeke after discovering his "best friend" had paid popular Presley to kiss Walker right in front of Lizzie.

Zeke had claimed he'd done it as a favor to Walker, insisting he'd overheard Lizzie telling Presley she'd used Walker to get to Zeke, since Lizzie was really into Zeke. It made sense. Zeke was the one the girls preferred. Not the tongue-tied, introverted Walker. But the fight and incident destroyed their friendship, and they'd never spoken again.

Conversely, Walker had tried explaining the whole thing to Lizzie, but she'd refused to speak to him. After she started dating Zeke, Walker had graciously bowed out of the picture and left for college in Nebraska. What difference would it make to tell her the truth now? The whole incident solidified Walker's resolve. Between Lizzie, Zeke, and his mother's desertion, Walker had developed the emotional barriers necessary to protect his heart from further rejection.

"Zeke was a hothead teen, and it's no surprise the relationship didn't work out between you two. You always were too good for him." The words escaped Walker's mouth before he realized it, and he inwardly cringed. "That was supposed to stay inside my brain." He offered a sheepish grin, expecting Lizzie to unleash her fury.

Instead, she smiled. "You're kind to say that. We've all grown up since high school, though, right?"

"Definitely." Eager to change topics, Walker shared a little about his time with the marshals and some of his old cases. They fell into calm conversation again, and he was grateful. But as he spent more time with her, Walker couldn't deny that Lizzie had become an amazing woman, inside and out. Regardless, Walker wouldn't destroy what they'd finally established. He hadn't made a move back then, and he wouldn't do so now—his only mission was to ensure her safety.

They talked until late in the night, and when Lizzie yawned, covering her mouth, he got the hint.

"It's almost midnight. I need to get to bed."

"Time flew by," Walker admitted, pushing to his feet.

"It was nice. We're required to check in at the command post before dawn."

"It'll be a quick night." Walker yawned, starting for the door.

Lizzie followed him. "Holler if you need anything."

"Will do." Walker exited the house and heard the lock click behind him.

He spotted the patrol unit parked in front of the house as he made his way to the apartment.

Walker kept the window blinds open and snagged a blanket and pillow. He dropped onto the sofa but kept watch for anything suspicious.

His thoughts revisited the escapees, somewhere out in the Colorado wilderness. Maybe watching them now. But with half of the Bison Valley PD and two deputy US marshals hunting them, they wouldn't enjoy their newfound freedom for long.

Walker replayed the night's conversation with Lizzie. He'd enjoyed the time with her, and to her credit, she'd been a gracious host. Strangely, he was comfortable around her. He had to remind himself they weren't friends, merely coworkers investigating a case.

But he couldn't help lingering on Lizzie. Her confidence and intelligence added to her beauty. What would things have been like if he'd had the courage to fight for her? Walker sighed and closed his eyes, allowing himself to drift off.

Unsure what woke him, he pushed off the couch, sitting upright.

Listening.

The hairs rose on his neck and arms, a visceral response.

Walker shoved away the blanket and glanced out the window. The rain had stopped, and darkness blanketed the grounds.

Not a sound.

And yet…his gut warned Walker something was wrong. Grateful he'd not taken off his boots, Walker snagged his duty weapon and headed for the door.

THREE

Lizzie gasped, unable to breathe. Panic jolted her fully awake, and pain coursed through her skull. Something completely covered her mouth, nearly eliminating the oxygen she could inhale through her nose. Her body moved, but her feet weren't touching the ground. Confused and disoriented, she whipped her head to the side, spotting the inverted landscape. The sun hadn't yet risen, and darkness encroached on every side. Her wrists were bound in front of her, giving her an advantage—and proof criminals were stupid.

A man carried her over his shoulder, based on the movement of his shoes below her. Lizzie tried screaming, only to realize the sound evaporated into the tape over her mouth. Her heart raced and she had to remind herself to breathe. If not, she'd hyperventilate and before the goon carrying her realized it, she'd pass out again. The throbbing headache rivaled a heavy metal band drum solo. *Slow breaths.*

Had he knocked her out before kidnapping her? The pulsating pain in her head testified to that supposition. Her next thought jumped to Reena. Where was her dog? Lizzie's heart thudded hard against her ribs as fear for her canine overrode her panic.

Reena never left her side. A memory in the periphery of her mind returned. Reena's muffled whines. She hadn't barked, warning Lizzie of an intruder. Had the man hurt or drugged her dog? Fury invigorated Lizzie, diverting her concentration from victim mode and into cop mode.

Unable to see him, Lizzie fixated on her surroundings, calculating which way to run when she escaped. Because she would escape.

The unfamiliar landscape solidified her fear that she wasn't on her property. She never ventured far from home, however, which didn't help her to mentally map her location. If they were on foot, that limited the distance and offered her hope. He couldn't carry her forever. Once they stopped, she'd make her move.

Lizzie wriggled her legs, affirming they weren't bound, which gave her the advantage. She was facedown against his back, the scent of perspiration filling her senses. He wore a black sweatshirt, which she'd guess was hooded to help disguise his face.

She tried to inhale, but the tape over her mouth compressed her nose and restricted air intake. The kidnapper paused and Lizzie took the opportunity. She pushed her bound hands against his back, lifting herself upright, then with full force, she brought her fists down, striking his kidneys. He groaned and his hold on her legs lessened slightly, giving Lizzie enough freedom to kick wildly.

Her efforts worked, and the man dropped her.

Lizzie landed with a hard thud on the rocky earth. She rolled to her knees and, using her bound hands, scooted backward, facing him.

"You'll pay for that."

She scoured him, mentally cataloging his full description. He wore dark jeans and a black hooded sweatshirt over a hooded black balaclava, completely concealing his face and head.

He stepped forward with the air of a stalker.

She interlaced her fingers, strengthening her attack.

His menacing form closed in.

Lizzie waited.

When he was within reach, Lizzie drove her fists upward, striking her intended mark. The man's hollered obscenities confirmed she'd succeeded. He bent over in pain, giving Lizzie space to jump up to her feet. She shoved against him, and he toppled to the ground, still groaning.

She spun and ran in the direction from where they'd come.

The uneven terrain made it difficult for Lizzie to sprint, and she fought to stay upright, refusing to be a horror-movie victim who stumbled over something and sprained her ankle.

Lizzie didn't look back. She'd not give him the satisfaction, but his heavy pants and hollered insults said he wasn't far behind.

Nothing about the area was familiar, and Lizzie struggled to decide which way to go. She ran forward with all her might and prayed it was the right direction.

In her concentrated efforts, she didn't anticipate his rear tackle. Unable to brace herself for the fall, she landed hard, slamming her chin onto an embedded stone.

The force whooshed the wind from her lungs and into the sticky tape over her mouth. Lizzie gasped, desperate to breathe.

The man got to his feet and jerked Lizzie up by one arm, nearly yanking her appendage from her shoulder. She cried out in muffled agony.

In a swift move, he tossed her over his shoulder again. She groaned at the impact, still trying to inhale.

Panic threatened to overtake her. Lizzie forced herself to stay calm and rationalize through the ache ratcheting in her chest and constricting her breaths. The crisp early morning air was calm. Crickets chirruped close by, indicating the rain had stopped. The man's footsteps were determined, quick. The ground whipped past her in a blur as he hastened his pursuit.

He hadn't killed her. Why? She knew the answer. He needed her alive. As bait? Or worse?

Then, in the distance, Lizzie heard the promise of help.

A bark.

Was she delusional?

Lizzie squeezed her eyes shut, silently begging God to lead Reena to her.

The man cursed under this breath and started to jog, confirming she'd not imagined her canine partner's barking. The shifting movement bounced Lizzie on his shoulder, and she feared the inverted motion would cause her to throw up.

He stopped as though listening. Lizzie mentally assessed her location. Her property butted against the foothills, which was where she surmised they were. She couldn't let him take her any farther. Whatever he had planned terrified her to the core.

Another yelp.

"Lizzie!" Walker's voice.

With a curse, the man dropped Lizzie again, and half her body splashed into cold water, drenching her legs and feet. The startling temperature caught her off guard. She twisted to see she was partially submerged in a creek.

The assailant stunned her with a kick to her side that shot horrendous pain through her chest and kept her from crying out. He repeated the action, and Lizzie was certain he'd cracked a rib.

She sucked in an excruciating breath, tucking her hands against her chest, then braced for another hit.

Instead, his footsteps faded as he fled. Lizzie opened her eyes, then pushed herself upward. She supported herself against a boulder and rose.

With an excruciating gasp, she ripped off the tape covering her mouth. Then, using every ounce of remaining strength, Lizzie screamed at the top of her lungs.

Without looking to see where her attacker had gone, Lizzie bolted toward Reena's barking. "Reena!"

Loud yapping responded.

"Lizzie!"

She fought the agonizing ache in her ribs and head, increasing her stride. At last, she spotted a flashlight beam bouncing ahead. The sight fueled her steps.

Reena and Walker met her halfway. Her dog protectively moved in front of her while permitting Walker to help.

"Lizzie!" Walker reached for her then, realizing her wrists

were bound, he withdrew a knife from his pocket. With one swipe, he cut through the tape, freeing her hands.

She stumbled backward, and Walker's strong grip caught her before she fell. He pulled her into his arms, and she didn't refuse the touch. Her body shook with the adrenaline dump and her teeth chattered.

"What happened? Who did this?" Walker didn't release his hold until Lizzie sucked in a life-giving breath, launching her into a coughing fit that nearly dropped her to knees.

She stepped back, wincing against the shooting fire piercing her ribs, and groaned.

"Are you okay?"

She nodded and gasped, holding her side. "He kicked me. I think he broke a rib. Or two."

Reena whined as though she understood, and Lizzie offered her a one-handed assurance.

"Okay. Hold on." Walker moved to a buddy-assist position, placing his shoulder under her armpit. "Lean all your weight on me." She did as he suggested, and they trudged slowly toward her house.

Once they crested the hill, she recognized her surroundings. Thankfully, the kidnapper hadn't taken her far from home.

"How did he get into the room, and where was Reena in all this?" Lizzie asked through gasps.

"A sound must've awakened me. I hurried downstairs and heard her whining and barking. I sort of barreled through your back door." He winced apologetically. "Reena was locked in your bedroom closet. I also rammed open that locked door."

"Thank you for finding her!" Lizzie said.

"You might not say that when you see the damage."

"How'd he get Reena into the closet?" Lizzie thought back to when she came to. "He must've drugged me or knocked me out while I was sleeping. I didn't even know that was a thing. But my head is raging." She looked at Reena, infuriated for any harm he might've caused her dog.

"I found a small tranquilizer dart on your bedroom floor," Walker said.

"And that explains why she didn't bark."

"I checked Reena, and she didn't appear to have any injuries," Walker said, as though understanding her concern.

When they reached the back side of her house, Lizzie saw her broken bedroom window and inspected the damage. She didn't touch the window-breaker tool that lay on the ground. Evidence technicians would need to document the scene. "And there's proof of how he got in."

Only the ambient porch light and Walker's flashlight illuminated the inky darkness that covered the landscape.

"Tell me everything you remember."

"I came to when I was already over his shoulder. I never saw his face. He had a black balaclava mask and hooded sweatshirt."

Walker shook his head. "Double disguise."

"He'd covered my mouth with duct tape before I awoke."

"Kudos for being stealth," Walker mumbled.

"No kidding." She hurried to the front door, Walker and Reena trailing. The patrol unit was absent. "Where is he?"

"Dunno. He wasn't there when I started searching for you."

"Fantastic." Lizzie led the way to the locked entrance.

"Back door," Walker said.

Lizzie hastened around the house, spotting the door hanging ajar by one hinge.

"Sorry about that," Walker said.

"No apologies necessary."

They entered through the kitchen. Clutching her side, she went straight to her bedroom and grabbed her cell phone, still plugged into the charger where she'd left it. Dialing Captain Cole, she dropped onto the edge of her bed. Walker stayed in the doorway.

Cole answered on the third ring, sounding groggy. "Lizzie?" he croaked.

She glanced at the clock and winced—2:45 glowed from the LED display. "Someone broke into my house and tried to abduct me." Lizzie launched into a full explanation, gasping over the pain in her ribs. She leaned, clutching her side. "If Walker and Reena hadn't come for me—" She didn't finish the thought, her body shivering involuntarily.

"Where's the cruiser?" Cole demanded.

"That was my first question, too."

"Are you injured? Have you called an ambulance or gone to the hospital for evaluation?" Cole pressed.

"I'm fine. My ribs are a little sore where he kicked me."

"You need to be examined by a doctor," Cole argued.

"No. There's nothing besides wrapping my side that the doctor will do. I can handle that here."

"Lizzie—"

"I promise I'll go if it gets worse," Lizzie negotiated.

"Okay." Cole didn't sound convinced.

"The weirdest part is that the intruder barely spoke." Lizzie redirected the conversation.

Walker moved closer, a quizzical look on his face.

"I'm on my way," Cole replied.

"Walker and I are holding down the fort," Lizzie insisted. "But I'd like to know why the patrol officer left."

"I will find out and arrange for evidence processing. Hopefully we'll get prints to identify the intruder. I'll be in touch."

"Thank you. I'll be fine," Lizzie assured him.

Cole disconnected after Lizzie promised him twice more that she and Walker could handle it.

"Your kidnapper barely spoke?" Walker asked.

"Yeah, a threat for hitting him, then he uttered a curse after I'd…" She hesitated, considering her words. "Hit him."

Walker gave a knowing glance. "Right. Well, that would do the trick."

"Wasn't enough to stop him, though."

Walker helped her to stand, and they headed for the kitchen. She dropped onto a chair, and he handed her an ice pack from the freezer. Lizzie placed it against her neck to alleviate some of the headache.

"Do you want me to wrap your side?"

"Not yet." The last thing Lizzie wanted was Walker doctoring her injury. Having him near and trying not to react was bad enough.

"If it was one of the convicts, my guess is he's a skilled fighter," he said. "They get a lot of practice in prison. Do you think he was worried you might recognize his voice?"

"It's possible." Lizzie shrugged. "I can't think past this headache. Mind if we relocate to the sofa?" Walker assisted her and she gently lowered herself onto the cushions, then stroked Reena, who remained glued to her side. "Thank you, Reena." Then, to Walker: "It's not like her to ignore any sounds. She barks at leaves, squirrels, the wind. Why didn't she alert?"

"He could've shot from a distance, using a long-range tranquilizer gun, then entered your room."

Lizzie shuddered. "After first breaking the window?"

Walker shrugged. "Or he had a partner, and they synchronized the attack."

Lizzie nodded. "One broke the window while the other delivered the shot. Reena didn't have a chance to bark before the dart hit her."

"Exactly, although it is strange that she didn't react to them being close to the house."

Reena whined as though apologizing. "You're a good girl. You rescued me." Lizzie kissed the dog's soft head. "Her bark scared him. Then you hollered. He dropped me and fled."

Walker sat beside her. His presence was strange but comforting. As much as her brain argued she should scoot away, her heart pleaded for his touch. She grabbed a throw pillow and hugged it before she did something emotionally unwise. "I'm glad you're here," she confessed.

"I'm sorry I didn't get to you sooner," Walker said.

"Whoever is out to get me won't stop." Lizzie's hands shook. "Why kidnap me instead of kill me?"

Walker wrapped the afghan around her shoulders, and she pulled it tighter. He didn't respond. He didn't need to.

Her phone rang again, with COK9 leader Emmett's contact information. "Wow, he must have a sixth sense or something." She answered on speakerphone, allowing Walker to eavesdrop on the discussion. "How'd you know?"

"Cole called me," Emmett replied. "Are you all right?"

"Yeah." Lizzie again provided a synopsis of the events.

"I'll send a couple of the closest task force members to help," Emmett suggested.

"No, it's okay. I have Deputy US Marshal Walker McCane here as an unasked-for bodyguard." Lizzie grinned at Walker, and he returned the gesture.

"I'm glad to hear that. If you require anything, we'll make it happen."

"I appreciate that."

"I hate to ask this—" Emmett began.

"Go ahead," Lizzie encouraged.

"Are you up for continuing on the case?" Emmett asked. "I understand if you need to heal—"

"I'm in. Absolutely." Lizzie sat up straighter as though to enforce her words.

"You're one of my best interrogators, so if you're up for it—"

"I am." Lizzie winced in embarrassment at interrupting Emmett.

"Good. Trevor will meet you tomorrow morning. I'd like you to interview Benny Fuller at the Oak City jail. He's had a little time to sit and simmer. Maybe he'll provide information about the adoption ring." The team had arrested Benny recently when he'd been caught attempting to abduct a young pregnant woman outside a free clinic in nearby Oak City. He was a known accomplice in the adoption operation, and they hoped he'd lead them to the mastermind behind it all.

Grateful he'd included her, Lizzie replied, "Roger that."

Walker's line rang and he excused himself to the dining room to answer the call.

"So far, Benny has refused to talk," Emmett said. "If anyone can get him to speak, it's you and Trevor. You two have great interviewing skills."

"Flattery will get you everywhere." Lizzie chuckled and grimaced through the pain. "We'll do our best."

"I have no doubt," Emmett replied. "Seriously, though, Lizzie, if you're not up for this—"

"I'm fine. Promise," Lizzie said. And she would be. No criminal would scare her away from her dream job.

"I'll take your word for it. If you need anything, don't hesitate to call."

"Will do." They disconnected.

Lizzie's hands trembled, but the headache had lessened. Her ribs were another story. Thankfully, interviewing a person of interest wouldn't require physical exertion. In fact, it provided a great excuse not to trudge through the wilderness on the manhunt.

She exhaled deeply, then checked Reena for wounds. "I'm sorry you got locked in the closet."

Reena's dark eyes peered up, begging forgiveness.

The sight tore at Lizzie's heart, and she hugged her dog. "It's okay. You'd never leave me voluntarily. You rescued me. I owe you my life." Tears welled in Lizzie's eyes.

Walker's returning footsteps got her attention and she swiped away the moisture and faced him. "I'll have our vet give her a full exam first thing in the morning," Lizzie said. "How did he render me unconscious?"

"Mind if I look?" Walker gestured to her neck, and Lizzie turned, pulling her long hair away from her nape. His strong touch sent a jolt through her, and she forced herself not to respond. "Yep, there's a small puncture wound."

"He injected me with something?" Lizzie's heart raced.

"If you're not feeling the effects anymore, I'd guess it's an anesthetic."

"Like ketamine," Lizzie grumbled. "Unbelievable."

"Yep, and doubtful you'd remember he administered the injection if that's what he used," Walker replied.

Lizzie swallowed down the fear threatening to overtake her reasoning. She searched her memory for anyone who'd want to hurt her and came up empty. Her pulse raced. If she couldn't identify her enemy, how would she stop him? He seemed to always be a step ahead of her. And why was he targeting her?

Walker shook his head at the text from Kelan. Running late. Be there soon.

"Late as always," Walker groused.

"Beg your pardon?" Lizzie asked.

"Kelan's on his way. If he'd gotten here sooner, your abduction might not have happened."

Lizzie waved off the comment. "There's no way to know that, and I'm sure he had good reason."

Walker ran his hand through his hair. "You're right. I'm tired and crabby." Truthfully, he blamed himself for not guarding Lizzie closer.

"With both of you here, I'll tell Captain Cole not to send another patrol officer. As if the last one did us any good."

"I appreciate it."

"With the escapees, Bison Valley PD is low on officers." Lizzie lifted her phone and made the call.

Walker returned to the evidence board. What were they missing?

Lizzie meandered into the room, still babying her side.

"You might reconsider having a doctor examine you."

"Negative. They'll just wrap it and send me home. I'm fine." She waved him off. "Cole was grateful you and Kelan would provide extra security." She gestured toward the board. "Any epiphanies?"

"Just reevaluating what we've already determined. The intruder has access to medications, which he used on you and Reena."

Reena gave a low growl.

"If I didn't know better, I'd say she understood me." Walker's gaze bounced between Lizzie and the canine.

"She probably does," Lizzie chuckled.

"Juhl and Arnold were dealers with the means to get drugs, including ketamine."

"Which adds to their motive," Lizzie replied. "But doesn't explain them targeting me since I have no connection to either."

"True." Walker crossed his arms and leaned against the table.

Reena barked and rushed to the front door. Headlights beamed through the curtains, and Walker withdrew his duty weapon from the holster on his hip. He approached, waving Lizzie down. She glared at him and followed, gun in hand. They flanked the window, and he peered out the side of the curtain, exhaling relief at the marked police unit.

"Evidence processing is here," Lizzie said.

Walker opened the door before the guy knocked, startling him. He flicked a glance at Lizzie. "Hey there, sorry—it's been a little stressful around here."

Walker studied the man, who wore a Bison Valley polo and cargo pants. He carried what Walker assumed was an evidence equipment box. Everything about him seemed legitimate. He shifted out of the man's way, permitting entry and earning him a wary look.

Lizzie tugged Walker's arm, and he stepped aside. "Come on in. The intruder entered through my bedroom window." She gestured down the hallway. "First door on the right."

Once the tech started for the room, Lizzie whispered, "Not sure what he'll find."

"Criminals are dumb, he might've left something."

"I'll talk with him."

"I'll conduct a perimeter check and watch for Kelan." Walker holstered his gun. "Hey, Lizzie?"

"Yeah?"

"Whatever it takes, we'll catch this guy," Walker promised, determination fueling him.

"Yes, we will." But doubt lingered in her eyes.

Worse, he couldn't shake the shame of letting her down. "I should've heard the intruder. The abduction never should've happened."

"That's not on you," she said.

He shrugged.

"If you don't mind, Reena would love an outside break, too. She doesn't need to be leashed—she'll stay close if you tell her to."

"Sure." Walker whistled and Reena stared at him.

Lizzie chuckled. "You'll have to call her."

"Oh, my bad. Come, Reena." The dog immediately trotted to his side. "Let's head outside." Reena wagged her feathery tail, and Walker opened the door.

He followed the K-9 to the back side of the house, where Lizzie's bedroom light glowed. He'd need to cover the window and repair the doors. Walker strolled the property, Reena trotting ahead of him, tail wagging as she sniffed the ground. The serene atmosphere transformed from terror into calm with Lizzie's return.

He recalled the gardening shed on the other side and hoped Lizzie had materials available to make temporary repairs. A padlock secured the doors. Relieved an intruder wasn't hiding out there, he turned and crossed the expansive lawn as headlights approached in the distance.

Reena sniffed along the shed, lingering.

"Reena," Walker called. She glanced over her shoulder as if to say, *What?* "Come on."

The dog hurried to him, and they waited near the driveway until Kelan's unmarked sedan had parked. The long gravel path allowed for two cars to sit side by side, and Kelan had wisely left room for the evidence technician's vehicle to exit.

Walker closed the distance between them. "That was fast."

Kelan unfolded from the car. The man's six-foot-four stature and linebacker build gave him an intimidating presence, at least to those who didn't know him. Kelan grinned wide as he emerged and Reena barked.

"He's okay," Walker assured. Facing his partner, he said, "This is Lizzie's tracking K-9, Reena."

"Hey, pretty girl." Kelan extended his hand, and Reena sniffed approval before moving to the evidence tech's vehicle. "Guess I've been accepted. Fortunately, this early, traffic was light." Kelan withdrew a duffel bag from the back seat. "Nice place."

"Yeah, and we're grateful for extra security." Walker updated Kelan on the events leading up to his arrival as they strode toward the front door.

"Wow." Kelan shook his head. "I leave you for one day and you're all out of control."

"What can I say?" Walker chuckled. "I need supervision."

"No harm in confessing the truth," Kelan teased, slapping him on the back.

Walker sobered. "How's my dad doing?"

"He's awesome. Doesn't love being under lock and key, but he's great about the whole situation."

"I appreciate you handling his relocation."

"Not a problem. I'll stop by again and check on him, too, and he's got twenty-four-seven protection."

"Good. Until we've established what or who we're dealing with, I need the reassurance he's safe. Especially with the perp tracking Lizzie down in her own home." Walker blew out a long breath. "I'll show you where we're staying." He led the way to the apartment.

"This is nice." Kelan set his bag on the table.

"You take the bedroom, I want to stay close to the door in case Lizzie needs help," Walker said.

"Works for me." Kelan carried his bag into the room, and then they headed back to Lizzie's.

"The intruder smashed up her bedroom window, and I had to ram a couple of doors. I'm hoping she's got supplies to secure them for tonight."

"Let's do it."

Walker opened the door, startling the evidence technician again. The guy stood on the opposite side and jumped back a foot, eyes wide. "Sorry about that." Poor dude was jumpier than a box of crickets.

The tech grumbled an incomprehensible remark and scurried past Walker. He glanced up, catching Kelan's amused grin, and shrugged. They entered the house, where Lizzie greeted them. "Hey, I'm Lizzie." She extended her hand, still gripping her side. "Rib," she offered in explanation.

"Kelan." He extended a beefy hand to her. "Thanks again for letting me crash here."

Lizzie smiled. "Not a problem."

"Walker updated me on the list of bizarre events y'all have dealt with. Gotta say, I agree. There's a connection here, we just need to find it." Kelan dropped onto the chair opposite Lizzie.

"Agreed," Lizzie said.

"Did the tech find anything?" Walker asked.

"Nope," Lizzie responded. "Not surprising, though."

"I'd prefer to temporarily fix the window and doors for tonight. Do you have any materials?"

"There's plywood in the shed out back."

"Great," Walker said. "Just need the padlock key."

To his surprise, Lizzie didn't argue. She withdrew a small key from a rack hanging near the back door and passed it to him. "Here you go."

"I'll help," Kelan offered.

They trudged outside and Walker located the supplies. "Tried to talk her into a visit at the hospital, but she refused."

"A broken rib is wicked painful," Kelan said. "But they can't do much but tape it."

"That's what she said."

Kelan grabbed the plywood, leaving Walker with the tools and nails.

"She's a nice lady," Kelan said.

"Yeah, we attended high school together."

"What? Did you know she worked here?"

"Nope, not a clue," Walker admitted.

"Didn't see a ring, either."

"I hadn't noticed." Not entirely untrue, he hadn't pressed about her current relationships.

"Hmm, interesting." Kelan propped up the wood over the window and Walker commenced securing it.

The made the repairs quickly, and when they'd finished, Walker showed him the whiteboard back at Lizzie's, filling him in on the possible connection between Juhl and Arnold as well as the access to drugs.

Kelan nodded. "I remember Juhl. Pretty nasty character."

They talked through the evidence and suppositions again, uncovering nothing new.

"I'm caught between needing sleep and being hungry," Lizzie

said. “It’s almost three thirty. I think I’m on a second wind or adrenaline rush.”

“I wouldn’t turn down food,” Kelan replied.

Walker laughed. “He never turns down a meal.”

Kelan shrugged playfully. “Ain’t no lie.”

“I’ll whip up something.” Lizzie excused herself to the kitchen, leaving Kelan and Walker alone.

“Between the manhunt and this case, you two have had your hands full.” Kelan dropped into a chair, consuming the seat with his massive frame. “Any ideas who created that list?”

“None.” Lizzie joined them with a plate of cheese and summer sausage.

“Between your pop and Lizzie, I can see the revenge thread,” Kelan said, sandwiching two pieces of cheese between slices of meat. “These convicts have too much time to conjure a plan. It’s possible the one targeting you rallied a few buddies willing to kill for fun.”

“I feel all warm and fuzzy,” Lizzie groaned.

“Sorry about that,” Kelan said good-naturedly.

As Lizzie and Walker filled Kelan in, the three devoured the cheese and sausage.

“Whew, I don’t know about you all, but I’m beat. I’ve been on the road nonstop for the past two days.”

“Me, too.” Lizzie got to her feet, collecting the empty plate and returning it to the kitchen.

“The apartment is great, but I didn’t hear the intruder from there,” Walker said.

Kelan looked around the room. “Maybe we should stake out here.”

Lizzie shrugged. “I’ll leave that up to you. There’s a spare room if you want to fight over it.” But if Walker wasn’t mistaken, she appeared relieved. “Bedtime, Reena.” The retriever sighed, slowly joining her partner.

Kelan laughed and Lizzie shook her head. "She's such a drama queen." She and the canine started toward the hallway.

"Hey, Lizzie?" Walker called.

"Yeah?" She faced them.

"Maybe you should sleep in the spare room," Walker said. "With that window compromised, it's not safe."

"Naw, I'll be fine," she reasoned, though her voice held no conviction.

"He's right," Kelan replied.

"Okay." Lizzie yawned again. "I'm too tired to argue." She waved and headed down the hall.

"Night," Walker and Kelan replied in unison.

"I'll crash on the sofa," Walker said.

"Oh, dude, I won't do that to you. I'm the freeloader. I'll take the couch," Kelan said.

"Naw, it's all good."

They parted, and Kelan strolled to Lizzie's room. Walker grinned, imagining the intruder's surprise at finding Kelan there instead of Lizzie. It would serve the kidnapper right if he returned.

Walker took his place on the sofa. Lizzie was more than capable, but he'd never forgive himself if something happened to her. Again. He offered a prayer of gratitude that he and Reena had found Lizzie when they did. Kelan's comment about Lizzie not wearing a wedding ring lingered, and Walker reminded himself that relationships were off-limits. The one he'd had had ended ugly, and he had no desire for a repeat. Too often he'd had to leave on short or no notice. And it wasn't fair to do that to anyone. No, he'd accepted his bachelor life and wanted to keep it that way. The thoughts jolted Walker into a reality check. He was here to do a job.

Satisfied he'd resolved the issue, Walker sprawled out on the sofa, glimpsing the clock. He wouldn't get much rest, but something was better than nothing. When his alarm woke him, he'd submerge himself in a cold shower and guzzle a gallon of hot coffee. Realistically, neither would suffice after the lack of sleep. But he'd take whatever help he could get, because they had to catch the escapees. One more night of sleeping feet away from Lizzie might send him over the edge.

FOUR

Walker swung hard, missing the hooded intruder. Sirens screamed in the distance, and he tried again, this time landing on something soft. No longer the offender, but now a pile of marshmallows. "What—" He blinked, staring at the pillow. Disoriented from the dream, he shot upright and surveyed the room. Slowly, the recollection of the hours before and Lizzie's house came into focus. He rubbed his face and shut off the offensive alarm on his cell phone, hoping he'd not woken Lizzie or Kelan. Then, swinging his legs off the sofa, he groaned and pushed to his feet.

The sun hadn't yet risen, but morning had arrived too soon. He walked down the hall and double-checked that both bedroom doors were closed before exiting through the garage and heading upstairs to freshen up. Walker finished getting ready as fast as possible and hurried back to Lizzie's house, entering through the garage to the kitchen where Kelan sat scrolling through his laptop.

"Good morning, sunshine," he greeted.

"Ugh." Walker ran a hand over his freshly washed hair. "I thought I'd be the first up and working today. What time did you get up?"

"About a half hour ago." He grinned. "I couldn't sleep. I kept thinking about the escaped convicts and trying to figure out any links to other cases we might've worked. Why were you and Lizzie on the kill list but I wasn't? We've partnered on several investigations while you and Lizzie haven't had any until now."

"And?" Walker poured a cup of coffee and dropped into the chair opposite Kelan.

"Nada."

"Thanks for making java." He lifted the cup, sipped and coughed. "Bro, that's awful."

Kelan laughed. "Sorry, I probably used too much."

"Ya think?" Walker took another swig and grimaced. "Although I'm dragging big-time, maybe the extra dose of caffeine will perk me up."

"Oh, in that case, you're welcome," Kelan joked. "Intravenous consumption might be better for you, but I didn't see medical supplies."

"I have a feeling it's going to be a long day."

The clicking of Reena's nails on the floor preceded the canine's entrance.

"Good morning," Walker greeted the dog.

She offered him a sniff before heading for the back door. Lizzie meandered behind, clutching her side.

Walker longed to help her but assumed she'd not welcome his touch.

"Morning," she uttered and seemed to study Walker and Kelan. "Did I oversleep?"

"Not at all," Walker replied. "Kelan made coffee." Ugh, his conversation skills were at an all-time brilliance.

"Bless you." Lizzie poured a cup.

He appraised her. Even with only a few hours of sleep, she looked fantastic, though her gait conveyed she was in pain. He averted his eyes, catching a smirk from Kelan before he resumed working on his computer.

She wore a dark green bulletproof vest sporting a Colorado K-9 Unit logo over a tan short-sleeved T-shirt and matching cargo pants. All of which fit her perfectly. Lizzie draped a windbreaker with the same emblem on the empty chair. "She beat me out of the bedroom." Lizzie crossed the room and opened the back door, releasing the dog, and gazed out the kitchen window. "Normally I let her roam in the morning, but I worry he might try to hurt her."

Walker nodded, interpreting "he" was the kidnapper. "How're you feeling?"

As though needing to prove it, Lizzie stood a little taller, but her face blanched. "Fine."

Walker's father had wisely told him when a woman said she was *fine*, it was a sure sign she wasn't. "You could rest—"

"Negative." Lizzie glared at him. "I've got work to do." She turned her back, permitting Reena inside. "I'll have to meet you guys at the command post. Our task force leader wants another officer and me to interview a suspect."

"No problem. I'll share my location with you, so you'll know where we're at," Walker said, lifting his phone and realizing he didn't have her contact information.

"Right." Lizzie crossed to him, took the device and entered her number. "There, now you have mine and I have yours." She handed him the device.

"We'd better get a move on." Kelan closed his laptop. "I need to grab a few things from my bag."

A knock sounded on the front door.

"That's Trevor." She set down her cup and rushed to answer, with Walker trailing.

Lizzie greeted an officer dressed similarly to her. "Deputy US Marshal Walker McCane, meet Lavender PD K-9 officer Trevor Slate."

The men shook hands.

"Where's Lark?" Lizzie inquired.

"That's my furry partner," Trevor explained to Walker. "I left her at the kennels for this. Hopefully, we don't need an arson-detection dog at the jail."

"Let's hope not." Lizzie yawned. "Short night."

"Emmett told me what happened." Trevor frowned. "How're you doing?"

"Just a little sore."

Kelan returned to the room, and Lizzie again provided introductions, and the men shook hands.

Walker's phone rang, and he glanced at the screen. "Hold up, Kelan. It's the boss." He swiped to answer on speakerphone. "Hey, I was about to call you. Kelan's here, too."

Lizzie gave him a thumbs-up and headed outside with Trevor, allowing the DUSMs privacy.

"You first," Supervisory Deputy US Marshal Kash Vandeaux said.

"We've had a few hiccups." Walker launched into a synopsis of the prior evening's events.

Kelan leaned against the wall.

"Glad you're both there," Vandeaux said.

Yeah, because I was such a tremendous help. The condemning thought came unbidden and delivered the gut punch Walker expected.

"I'll call the command post next to update them. We captured two of the escaped convicts, Steve Gossard and Thornton Pfeiffer, early this morning."

"That's incredible." Walker and Kelan engaged in a fist bump. "Any chance either of them is Lizzie's attempted kidnapper?"

"Nope. They were busy trying to hold up a gas station in Denver last night," Vandeaux said. "It went bad, but law enforcement neutralized the situation and apprehended both with no casualties."

"When did this happen?" Kelan asked.

"The whole thing started at twenty-two hundred," Vandeaux replied, referencing 10:00 p.m. military time.

"Hmm. Lizzie's attack occurred after midnight," Walker said.

"So can't be them," Vandeaux added. "As far as the prison bus ambush, neither is talking nor confessing to anything."

"Out of stubbornness?" Kelan inserted.

"Partially," Vandeaux said. "But after interviewing them, my guess is they fear retribution."

"Which confirms there's a person on the outside helping them," Walker said.

"Or at least someone higher up the criminal food chain calling the shots," Vandeaux said.

"We suspect whoever orchestrated the ambush must be familiar to the convicts or has a respected reputation," Kelan added. "Unless we're missing it, there's no direct link to all of them."

"Good work," Vandeaux agreed. "Right now, units are transporting them to the jail in Oak City."

"That's where Lizzie and Trevor Slate are interviewing a suspect in an unrelated case," Walker explained.

"I'm in communication with Emmett Dane at COK9, so I'm aware of the situation."

"Why take the convicts to a small-town detention center?" Walker glanced at the clock. Fear for Lizzie's safety overrode everything tumbling around in his brain. Surely they wouldn't intersect with the prisoners. "Sir, maybe we should reconsider."

"Negative. That's the only option," Vandeaux said. "Advise Lizzie regarding the transport unit. They're already en route, and it's the jail closest to Bison Valley. The good news is it's a temporary arrangement until we can transfer them to Cañon City, where they were supposed to go before the ambush."

"Understood."

"However, if you feel that strongly about Lizzie coming into contact with the prisoners, perhaps she should reconsider protective custody." Vandeaux added, "Especially after the attack last night."

Walker cringed. His suggestion had done the exact opposite of what he'd intended. Now Vandeaux would think she was incapable. "Negative, sir. She's working a case for COK9 and unwilling to let criminals force her into hiding."

"Can't blame her." His boss sighed. "Can't force her."

"Exactly."

"We got this," Kelan injected.

Walker shot his friend an annoyed glance.

Vandeaux chuckled. "I've no doubt, Kelan."

"We'll ensure her safety," Walker assured his boss.

"You two are my best. I have full confidence you'll handle it. Keep me updated and I'll do the same."

They disconnected.

"You want me to accompany Lizzie to Oak City?" Kelan offered.

Lizzie would strangle him if he suggested it, but he'd at least give her the heads-up. "Let me handle it."

They exited the house and approached Lizzie and Trevor. Walker couldn't shake his concern about leaving her unprotected.

"My boss said they captured two of the convicts, Gossard and Pfeiffer, and are transporting them to the Oak City jail," Walker explained.

"Any chance—" Lizzie began.

"Nope, they were busy holding up a gas station while your kidnapper was in action," Walker said.

"Then they weren't involved in my attack," Lizzie concluded.

"My guess is all these convicts are *involved*," Kelan said, earning him agreement from the group.

"Be careful, Lizzie," Walker said.

She held his gaze, and Kelan glanced between them. "All right. Time to hunt fugitives." He strolled to his unit.

"Hey, Walker." Lizzie gestured toward his SUV. He approached, and she pointed to his flattened tires.

Trevor shook his head. "Unbelievable."

"Nice," Walker growled. "Wonder if that happened last night when the kidnapper came to the house or afterward."

Lizzie shrugged. "No clue."

The idea sprouted and eased Walker's concerns regarding his and Lizzie parting. "On second thought, mind if I tag along with you?"

"Why?" Lizzie quirked a brow.

"I'll watch the vehicles while you're conducting the interview," Walker said. Based on Trevor's smirk, it sounded weak.

"Walker, I don't need a personal bodyguard."

"Lizzie, you're recovering from the attack. There's no shame in that. And based on the way you're babying your side, you're still in pain."

She frowned and exhaled. "Curse you and your X-ray vision," she teased.

He smiled. "That's the spirit. Really, we can't be too careful. The kidnapper tried to carjack you once."

"You win this round."

"Thanks." He texted Kelan the new plan and his friend responded with a thumb-up emoji. Then Walker rushed to his vehicle and withdrew the bag of snacks he kept in the console along with his phone charger.

"Are you sure you don't want to simply get your tires replaced?" Lizzie knelt to look at the damage. "I don't know how long this will take." She rose.

"No worries. I came prepared." He held up the bag of potato chips he'd absconded with from his unit.

She screwed up her face in disgust. "At 0600?"

"What? Hash browns are potatoes, right? It's just in a different form." Trevor seemed to watch the exchange, amusement in his expression.

Lizzie laughed and winced, holding her side as she unlocked her vehicle. "It hurts to laugh."

"I could drive," Walker offered.

Trevor shook his head as if to say, *Don't even try it, dude.*

"Not sure Cole would appreciate me handing over my automobile to the marshals," Lizzie quipped. "It's all good."

Could she be anymore stubborn if she tried? Her unrelenting expression told Walker not to bother arguing.

"We'll follow you," Lizzie said. A text chimed on her phone. "Carly will meet us at the jail. She'll examine Reena while we're interviewing Benny." Carly Mayor was a veterinarian who'd recently started dating their colleague, Officer Eli Blackwood.

Trevor gave a jerk of his chin and headed for his unit.

They loaded up, and she followed Trevor.

Vandeaux's words looped in Walker's mind. *Glad you were there.* His job last night had been to protect Lizzie, and still the intruder had invaded her home and kidnapped her. The creep had even drugged Reena, all while Walker had slept.

He'd not give the criminal a second opportunity.

Lizzie was grateful that Walker had insisted on coming with her, though she'd never admit it. The soreness in her ribs had hindered her movement, but she'd not give anyone reason to think her incapable of performing her job duties. If she'd relented and allowed Walker to drive, Captain Cole or Emmett might use it as a justification for dismissing her from the cases. That would not happen. *Suck it up, buttercup.*

"Thank you for allowing me to tag along," Walker said.

"It'll work well for Reena, too. I never leave her behind, but she doesn't need to be in the interview with us."

They traveled quietly, neither speaking until they reached Oak City.

She parked and they hopped out. Lizzie rushed to Trevor's unit when she saw a text from Emmett, eliciting his raised eyebrow and concerned expression as Trevor opened the driver's door. "Emmett's got an update for us."

Trevor's face relaxed with evident relief, and they returned to her unit, allowing Walker to listen. Lizzie called the COK9 team leader back. "Hi, Emmett." She placed the call on speakerphone.

"The DNA sample expedited from the adopted Taylor infant is not one of the victims' babies."

"A double-edged sword for sure," Lizzie said.

"Great news for the Taylors," Trevor replied.

"I'd like to notify them, if that's acceptable?" Lizzie asked.

"Absolutely. Let me know how the interview goes." Emmett disconnected.

Lizzie offered a silent prayer for the stolen infants and their mothers as she excused herself to call the Taylors. Mrs. Taylor was overjoyed to hear the news that the DNA wasn't a match for one of the victims, while her husband seemed annoyed, saying they'd known all along. After Marina thanked her profusely, Lizzie hung up and headed back to the SUVs.

Lizzie faced Walker and handed him the keys. "Reena should be fine in her kennel, but just in case."

"We'll spend the time getting acquainted." Walker scratched the dog between her ears.

"You'll win her heart that way," Lizzie said. She gestured at the chips. "Don't you dare feed that junk to her."

Walker blinked, feigning innocence. "I wouldn't dream of it."

"I mean it."

"Is she allergic?"

"No. But she's not allowed people food." Lizzie narrowed her eyes.

"Okay."

Carly pulled up beside Lizzie's unit and exited her car.

"Thanks for doing this on the go."

"Not a problem," the blue-eyed brunette replied. "If Reena hasn't exhibited issues, she's probably fine. I'll take a blood sample and call you if I have concerns."

"No news is good news, right?"

"Exactly."

She and Walker waited as Carly performed the exam, which went quickly. After the vet had driven away, Lizzie withdrew the case file from her door panel. "Be back soon."

Walker ripped open the bag and popped a chip into his mouth. "We'll be here."

She wagged a finger at him in final warning, then closed the door and met Trevor.

"Do we have a game plan for this?" he asked.

"Not really."

"Maybe a little bluffing will get Benny talking," Trevor suggested.

"You lead, I'll follow."

The duo entered the jail and identified themselves to the guards on duty, who led them to the weapon lockers, where they secured their service pistols before walking into the interview room. The narrow space contained a rectangular table in the fashionable gunmetal gray that most government-issued furniture came in, along with two matching chairs. Lizzie studied the man seated across from her. Benny Fuller, tall and skinny with dirty-blond hair and lifeless light blue eyes, stared at them.

Trevor took the seat closer to the wall.

"I'm Officer Reynolds, and this is Officer Slate," she introduced, sliding into the open chair and placing the case file on the table out of Benny's reach.

"Benny, I'm sure you understand why we're here," Trevor began.

"Yeah, and it doesn't matter," Benny replied.

"Right now, you're most likely the one facing jail time for the murders of three innocent women, the abduction of their three newborn babies and the kidnapping of Mia Andrews," Trevor said.

Lizzie watched Benny's expression and body language at Trevor's bluff.

"I didn't kill nobody." Benny leaned back, looking bored.

"But you know who did?" Lizzie asked.

"Nope." Benny clamped his mouth shut, working his jaw. He averted his eyes, pretending to study something intriguing on the ceiling.

Lizzie tossed in a little more bait. "And if Mia delivers her baby, we'll add to the charges of a fourth abducted infant."

"No way!" Benny jerked upright against his restraints.

Lizzie and Trevor shared an interested glance at the man's reaction.

A slight sheen covered Benny's forehead. "That's not on me, man."

"But it is. Unless you give us something more to go on," Trevor replied.

Lizzie leaned forward. "Come on, Benny. If you have information, now is the time to tell us. Otherwise, you're looking good for all those charges based on your attempt to kidnap a woman outside the free clinic. Fits the MO to a T."

Benny shook his head, and Lizzie noticed his carotid artery thumping hard in his neck. He was nervous, with sufficient reason. But she wanted the cause. Guilt for the crimes he'd committed or another matter?

Lizzie withdrew pictures of the victims and pushed them closer to Benny. His breaths came out harder and faster, and again averted his eyes. His body language conveyed anxious energy. She and Trevor were getting to him. Good.

"It's looking bad, Benny," Trevor said. "I'd start talking if I were you." He crossed his arms in a silent standoff.

Benny chewed on his lower lip. "Man, you don't get it." He lowered his voice to a whisper, forcing both to lean in to hear. "I can't say anything, or Trigger will kill me." His eyes widened as if he hadn't meant to speak that name. Lines of concern creased his damp forehead. "I can't talk. I just…can't."

"Who's Trigger?" Lizzie pressed.

Benny shook his head. "Nuh-uh. No way."

"I guess we could ask around." Lizzie shrugged. "I've got CIs who might recognize the name."

"If your CI wants to live, they won't say nothing about Trigger." Benny snorted. "You won't get any information from anyone."

"Why are you so afraid of him?" Lizzie asked.

Benny looked at her, his gaze unwavering.

"We could mention to the CI that Benny referenced Trigger," Trevor said.

"No, please don't!" Benny's gaze flicked from left to right as though Trigger would appear out of nowhere. "I would tell you, but he'll kill me. Please."

Trevor attempted several more times to press Benny, but he'd clammed up tighter than a Tupperware lid. When it became apparent they'd get nothing more out of him, Lizzie and Trevor exited the room.

Once they were outside, she said, "It's a beginning. Let's have Eva check into the name Trigger."

"Finally, new data," Trevor agreed. "At least this wasn't a complete waste of time."

"Definitely. I wonder if Trigger is the leader of this ring that we've needed from the start." Lizzie called the team's tech analyst, and she promised to do some digging and get back to them.

"I'm thrilled we have a lead," Lizzie said after she'd disconnected.

Trevor seemed distracted.

"Hey, everything okay?"

"Yeah." His creased forehead and furrowed brows said otherwise.

Lizzie waited for him to elaborate. When he didn't, she said, "I'm a good listener if you want to talk."

"Sorry, I'm lost in my own world. Dealing with my mom. She's been living with me, but she requires more care than I can provide," Trevor explained. "It's a lot to deal with."

"Oh, I'm sorry. Is there anything I can do?"

"No." Trevor stepped forward. "Thanks for the offer, though."

Lizzie smiled, her heart going out to him. "Okay. I'll head over to the manhunt now."

Trevor nodded and strolled to his vehicle.

Lizzie slid behind the wheel of her own SUV, joining Walker inside. "How'd it go?"

"Reena thinks I'm amazing," Walker said.

Lizzie narrowed her eyes at him. "You fed her potato chips, didn't you?"

"What?" Walker blinked again with a feigned innocent look.

"Walker McCane." Lizzie shook her head and started her engine. "We might've gotten a lead. It's thin, but we have an alias or nickname for someone calling the shots."

"Hey, whatever pushes you forward counts," he encouraged. "Do you and Trevor need to make any more stops?"

"Nope, let's shift gears and brainstorm how we made it onto a kill list while we hunt for the rest of the escapees."

"Multitasking cases is my fave," Walker quipped. "I hate to say this, but it's all been a little too quiet."

"Seen anything suspicious?"

"No, but my gut says otherwise. Let's just stick close together."

"Roger that." Lizzie informed Trevor, and he agreed to lead them out of the area.

"So, you're chasing this Trigger person?" Walker asked.

"Possibly. But I'm confident we're getting closer to busting the ring. Now, if we could figure out who was out to kill me, I'd really feel better."

"We will," Walker assured her.

They left the jail in a caravan line and, once out of Oak City, turned onto a side road.

Walker glanced out the passenger mirror. "I don't like this. There's nothing but trees and rocks around here."

"It's great for getting away from the busyness of the city, but not so much for recon." Lizzie radioed Trevor. "Move to a secure channel," she advised.

"What's up?" he asked.

"Keep watch and I'll stay close until we get to the command post."

They'd driven another couple of miles when Reena poked her head through the divider.

"Hey, girl," Walker said, stroking the dog.

She emitted a low growl, and he quickly withdrew his hand. "What did I do?"

"It's not you." Lizzie surveyed the desolate area, foothills rising on both sides of the two-lane road. "Hey, Reena's acting strange," she radioed. "Be on the watch."

Reena stayed close, clearly on edge.

"Dark SUV four o'clock," Trevor reported, and his brake lights flickered as he decelerated. "Stop sticks!"

Lizzie slammed on the brakes in time to see Trevor's SUV bounce over the deflation device someone had placed on the road. The black line of hollow prongs punctured all four tires. Trevor swerved, veering off the road.

"It's a trap," Trevor said. "Keep going, I'll call for backup." He pulled to the side.

"I'm not leaving you," Lizzie radioed.

"Go!" Trevor shouted. "Get out of here."

Lizzie reluctantly accelerated, swerving around the long spiked line, and simultaneously closed the divider door to keep Reena protected in her kennel.

An SUV peeled out from the right side of the road and sped past Trevor and toward her.

"They're not interested in him. They're after you," Walker said, withdrawing his weapon.

The SUV revved, closing the gap.

"Get down!" Walker yelled.

Lizzie ducked but kept her eyes on the road. "There's no place to make a U-turn."

"Just go, create distance."

Rapid gunfire pelted around them, piercing the SUV's body and shattering Walker's side mirror. He rolled down his window and leaned out, returning fire.

Lizzie swerved, catching a bullet in the rear passenger tire. "We're hit."

The gunshots continued, but Lizzie felt the tug of the vehicle. "I won't be able to go much farther."

"Can you get to that corner?"

"Yes." Lizzie fought for control, doing as Walker suggested. She skidded near a copse of massive evergreens and slammed into Park. Lizzie released Reena, and they fled her unit, running for the cover of the forest.

With hand signals, she and Walker sought better shelter. The shooting stopped, but as they hid behind a row of low brush, Lizzie spotted a man hurrying toward them with a gun at the ready.

Walker fired, but the man ducked in time. Now they'd signaled the shooter to their hiding spot. He disappeared behind a huge boulder and returned fire. Then he was moving again.

"He's coming toward us," Lizzie whisper-yelled. "No, he's fleeing!"

The assailant shifted, running deeper into the wilderness, where the thick foliage hindered their visual tracking.

Lizzie rose, surveying the area but unable to see where the shooter had fled.

"We can't let him get away!" Lizzie urged Walker to follow her. "Reena can track him."

"Lizzie." Walker shook his head. He glanced at the dog, skepticism in his expression.

"I'm going with or without you," Lizzie replied. "It's not an option." She got to her feet, keeping Reena's lead tight to her side, and started after the shooter.

Her boots crunched on the pine needles and dead leaves littering the ground, but the birds had stopped singing as though they sensed the danger.

The sun peeked through the overhanging trees, shadows flickering all around them and straining Lizzie's vision. Walker gestured to a thin trail between large fir trees. She nodded understanding and Reena confirmed it by moving toward the space.

As they ventured into the thickening woodland, the path became less prominent. Reena sniffed a trail ahead of them, and Lizzie gave her the full length of her leash. She trusted her dog.

A branch snapped from somewhere close by and Lizzie tugged the lead. Walker squatted beside her, and they waited.

The sound of a mosquito invaded the silence, buzzing near her ear, and Lizzie shooed it away with her hand. After several seconds, Walker rose and she followed, again gesturing for Reena to track the shooter.

Lizzie swiped at the low-hanging branches that scraped her face. Walker was beside her, gun at the ready. How far had they gone? Lizzie glanced over her shoulder, hoping they'd be able to backtrack their way out of the forest.

Reena paused, sniffing the air and the ground. She moved to the right, repeating the actions. With Lizzie's guidance, Reena urged them farther into the woods.

The climb was strenuous, and Walker's forehead shone with perspiration from the exertion. She could only imagine what she looked like. Her leg muscles screamed, and her ribs were on fire, but she'd not give in. Not now. They were closing in on him. She just knew it.

Without warning, gunshots pinged all around them.

They ducked, and Lizzie tugged Reena close. The group again took cover, hovering behind a boulder.

"The shots seemed to come from everywhere and nowhere at the same time," Lizzie hissed.

"Yeah. It's the forest, reverberating the sound," Walker replied.

Lizzie contemplated their options. If they pressed onward, was she endangering Reena? But what if they didn't? They might not get another opportunity to track the shooter, and it was clear he wouldn't stop.

They risked being hit, but they couldn't let the guy escape. Not when they were so close.

The shots stopped. He was running again.

Walker and Lizzie exchanged a nod, confirming they'd press on, and rose from their hiding place.

"Let me go ahead of you," Walker whispered.

"You can't." Lizzie shook her head. "Reena has to lead."

"Right." Walker frowned. "Okay, I've got your six."

They got into formation again, hiking through the forest in search of signs to where the assailant had gone.

A twig snapped from the side, and the group froze.

Without warning, rapid fire exploded around them.

Reena yelped.

Lizzie lunged to shield the retriever and prayed she wasn't hurt.

FIVE

Walker dived for Lizzie, falling short as he rolled away from shots pelting the ground. His mind wrestled to comprehend the situation, categorizing the protocol for his next move.

Lizzie pinned Reena down, shielding the dog with her body.

"Are you hit?"

"No, but not sure about Reena."

Walker covered his head, gaining his bearings. Through the mass of foliage, he struggled to spot the shooter's location. Loud pops pierced the air, confusing his senses.

A foot ahead, Lizzie scooted Reena behind a grouping of shrubs.

He army-crawled toward them, bullets pelting the tree trunks overhead. "Is she hurt?"

Lizzie frantically ran her hands through Reena's thick fur. "I don't know." The panic in her voice sent dread radiating through Walker. "Cover us."

Walker scurried behind the bramble in front of Lizzie and periodically glanced at her. The shadowed atmosphere made it hard to see her progress with Reena.

More shots.

Walker returned fire then ducked again.

Lizzie combed through Reena's fur and the dog remained calm, although shock might mask that reaction. Smatterings of branches flicked Walker's face, and he dropped lower. A huge rock to his right offered better concealment. "Lizzie, on my count, move there." He gestured toward the stone, and she nodded.

Walker peered up, then said, "One, two—" On *three*, they

dashed across, Walker shooting in a counterattack. Once secured, he asked, "Find anything?"

"Something is stuck in her paw." Lizzie examined her dog, tilting her paws upward into the light.

Walker fired twice, then crouched beside her again.

"Got it!" she exclaimed, holding up the offensive thorn.

Another blast above them sobered Lizzie's enthusiasm, and she shrank close to him.

Walker reciprocated, emptying his magazine with fury. The assault resulted in momentary silence. He snapped in the second magazine he carried in his cargo pants pocket. "Stay low," he advised. "I've searched the area, but the trees and leaves shadow everything. I can't pinpoint exactly where the shots are originating."

"It seems like he's moving forward."

"Running away for sure."

Several more rounds filled the air, halting their conversation.

When the shots ceased, Walker suggested, "Maybe we should head back. We don't know what's on the other side of this forest. The remaining escapees might be waiting to ambush us."

"True." Lizzie bit her lip, deliberation written in her expression. "But right now there's only one. And if we don't pursue him, we may not have another opportunity. No way. We've come this far. We're not giving up."

Walker regarded her, amazed and impressed at her resolve while terrified she might get hurt. But Lizzie was no damsel in distress. She was holding her own. With a sigh, Walker acquiesced. He couldn't argue her reasoning, but the unknowns mounted against them.

Suddenly another round of bullets bounced off the ground near the boulder and overhead on the tree trunks.

Neither moved and only Reena's panting filled the space between them.

At last, the gunshots ceased, leaving only the soft rustle of trees. Walker and Lizzie each took a side and peered around their protective barrier.

Walker lifted his hand, requesting Lizzie wait, allowing him to go first. She touched his left shoulder, acknowledging the action. He slowly crept to the edge, seeking the shelter of the brush, then inched forward, moving from evergreen to conifer.

A squirrel scampered out from a bush and darted to the oak tree across from him, bounding upward and into the thick leafy branches. "Where are you?" he whispered to himself, searching for the assailant and wishing he had binoculars.

Once Walker confirmed that a gun wasn't aimed at him with the criminal lying in wait, he gestured for Lizzie to follow.

She took the lead, Reena sniffing the path forward. Walker stayed behind the team, and they proceeded in a stack position through the forest. They reached a narrow creek, and Reena paced the bank. Had she lost the scent?

The rustle of leaves gained Walker's attention, and he twisted to the left, catching the white fluff of a rabbit's tail as it bounded into shrubbery. There, he spotted a space between broken branches. "Wait," he whispered.

Lizzie paused, and he crossed over the water toward the thicket. When he saw the telltale sign of their shooter, he waved Lizzie over. She and Reena joined him, and he gestured to boot prints embedded in the ground. "Will this help?"

"I'm offended you had to ask," she teased, then to the dog, she indicated the earth and ordered, "Find."

Reena sniffed the place, and Lizzie repeated the command. With a lunge, Reena took off, surprising them by squeezing between thick bushes.

The sharp branches and thorns tore at Walker's pants and shirt, but the retriever was on a scent, and they didn't pause. Instead, Walker and Lizzie jogged to keep up.

Walker feared their approach made too much noise, but Lizzie didn't hesitate. When a clearing appeared, they paused with

Lizzie restraining Reena. Walker shifted in front of them and spotted a structure farther in the distance, tucked among several pine trees.

With a confirming nod, they stepped out of the forest shelter and hurried across the meadow. Approaching the grungy old fishing cabin, Walker couldn't determine whether it was abandoned or had simply seen better days.

They aimed for the windowless side, hoping to make a stealth approach. Razor wire surrounded the property, forcing them to step carefully around the dangerous barrier. In his peripheral vision, Lizzie motioned to Reena in what he assumed were silent commands.

Once they reached the lodge, Walker asked, "Think he's in there?"

"Reena seems to think so. Or at least he was. But there's only one way to answer that question."

Right. They had to enter the cabin. Walker grunted. "Yeah, unless he shoots us while we're trying."

"Ready when you are," she cooed sarcastically.

They stayed in the shadows, flanking the dwelling. Careful to steer clear of the windows and door, they rounded the structure to the front.

Walker motioned that he'd go first, ducking beneath a cobweb-covered window beside the wooden door. He bobbed low, then peeked through the glass, shielding his eyes with one hand, and visually scanned the interior. The living space appeared empty. He signaled for Lizzie to join him and together they climbed the two decayed and crumbling porch steps and approached the entrance.

Lizzie motioned to Reena, and the dog shifted into a guard stance. With both standing, backs flat against the log walls, Walker mouthed, *One, two—*

On *three*, he kicked open the door, bursting inside, gun at the ready. Lizzie followed and they cleared the house with a quick sweep. A confined bathroom no larger than a coat closet was the only other room.

"Reena," Lizzie called.

A couple of raggedy armchairs and a card table completed the sparse décor, and the kitchenette to the side held a coffeemaker and empty soup cans.

"Check this out." Walker located a prison-issued jumpsuit tucked into the cushion of a chair.

"Confirms an escapee was holing up here." Lizzie captured pictures of the garment with her cell phone before Walker carefully pried it out, using a pen from his pocket.

"Why would he lead us here and then take off?"

"I don't think he intended for us to follow," Walker said. "The shift in his direction was the long way. He probably tried veering off course, assuming Reena wouldn't track him through the creek. I'm guessing he had another mode of transportation hidden here."

"We didn't hear an engine," Lizzie argued. "Although that doesn't exclude him walking a motorcycle out to the road or driving an electric car."

"Exactly."

She gestured toward the clothing. "Do they mark the jumpsuits with identifiers specific to the inmate?"

"Nope, standard issue to every convict."

"Ugh." Lizzie turned, visually surveying the space. "So where is he now?"

"And the bigger question is, if he's not alone, will they return?"

"I'd rather not find out."

"Definitely. Let's head back. Unless someone else has a dog as skilled as Reena, I'm not sure anyone would discover us here."

"Agreed." Lizzie held up her phone. "Of course, there's no cell service."

"Does that surprise you?" Walker gestured at the decrepit surroundings.

"Not in the least."

They started out, taking the same path as Reena led.

"You were a force to be reckoned with," Walker commended.

"I just hold the leash. Reena does the work." Her smile lit up the darkened forest and Walker struggled to keep from pulling Lizzie into his arms. Everything about her had him hooked, worse than when they were in high school. She was amazing. Without warning, images of them dating and all the possibilities for a future bounded to mind. And in the forest's serenity, with Lizzie in the lead, Walker allowed himself time to ruminate.

"You're too quiet back there," Lizzie said.

Her voice jerked him to the present, and he shook off the irrational dreams. "My brain is racing."

"I hear that."

The return trip went much faster, with familiar landmarks assisting in their trek. Once they reached her vehicle, Lizzie radioed for backup. To their surprise, units arrived within minutes.

Trevor exited one police car. "We were already heading this way when you called," he explained.

"I figured you were talented at finding me," she kidded.

While they waited for the tow trucks to haul the suspect's and Lizzie's vehicles, Walker and Lizzie updated their respective bosses via phone. Trevor told them the SUV the suspect drove had been reported stolen by the owner earlier that morning.

Vandeaux added that he'd arrange for evidence techs to collect the prison garb and run it for DNA. Walker and Lizzie concluded that the clothing's condition made identification of an escapee unlikely.

Though they'd narrowed their list of suspects, neither boss had discovered more clues to pinpoint which criminal was responsible for the attack.

Walker watched Lizzie talking with Trevor, aware his feelings for her had returned full force. If he was honest with himself, he'd admit they'd never gone away. He swallowed hard. It didn't matter. He didn't intend to pursue Lizzie or anyone else. Because deep down, those wounds lingered, with the images of Zeke and Lizzie together, then JoLynn walking out on him. Walker shoved aside the thoughts. He wasn't an insecure teenager anymore. His job required his full attention in recovering the escapees. Lizzie wouldn't be safe until he did.

"Ready?" she asked, jolting him from his internal contemplations.

They climbed into a police cruiser and rode back to her place.

"My boss will have the SUV repaired and brought to us in a few hours," she explained. "Between my rig and Trevor's, we've taxed resources."

Once they reached her house and settled inside, Lizzie said, "I need to freshen up and get all the grunge off me."

"I'll work on something to eat," Walker replied.

"Thanks."

While Walker pulled together a simple meal of chicken salad, Reena snoozed comfortably in her dog bed in the living room. It felt natural to be with Lizzie, as though they belonged.

But they didn't, and he'd have to remind himself of that fact a lot if he expected to survive this case with her without confessing his feelings.

Lizzie entered the kitchen, her long hair wet and combed away from her face. She wore sweatpants and a T-shirt, looking incredibly beautiful. "Oh yum, I love chicken salad," she said, taking a seat at the table.

"My turn to clean up. Don't wait for me." Walker excused himself, desperate for distance from Lizzie. He rushed up to the apartment, relishing the hot water that eased the soreness in his muscles. He allowed himself to relax.

When he returned to the living area, Lizzie lounged on the sofa watching TV. "I needed something brainless."

"Works for me." He pulled together a sandwich and joined her.

"That wasn't the day I expected," Lizzie said.

"Me, either." Walker's phone chimed with a text. "Kelan should be here in about half hour—he said he's bringing pizza."

"He just became my best friend," Lizzie teased.

"Mine, too—that chicken salad wasn't enough." He shifted position on the couch and glanced out the window. A Bison Valley PD cruiser was parked in front of the house.

"I've wanted to ask you something."

Walker reverted his attention to Lizzie. "Sure."

"Why did you invite me to prom if you really liked Presley?" As though hearing the words for the first time, she added, "I'm not upset. Anymore. I'm curious."

Walker's pulse pounded in his ears. Two things occurred to him at that moment. One, Zeke had never told her the truth about that night, and two, Lizzie blamed him for the whole fiasco. Kudos for her wanting to deal with the relationship rhinoceros in the room, but dread coursed through him at the discussion.

Her piercing gaze said she wasn't letting him off the hook.

"No amount of apologizing will fix what happened that night, but for what it's worth, I'm really sorry." He'd not expound on the reasons. They wouldn't matter in the long run, and it'd sound like he was trying to justify the situation and blame Presley for kissing him. Besides, after that, Zeke and Lizzie had become a couple, confirming Zeke's claim of her attraction to him. Everything had worked out the way it was supposed to.

"We were young and made immature kid choices." Lizzie appeared a little disappointed, but she pushed to her feet. "I need to give Reena a potty break." She headed for the door and Walker grabbed his duty weapon, escorting her outside.

Birds chirped, and the air smelled fresh. Walker thought about telling her the whole truth, but decided the result would be the same. Would she reconsider dating another law enforcement person? Someone like him? Maybe they could have a second chance.

Walker opened his mouth just as Kelan's SUV pulled in the

driveway, reminding him romance was out of the question. Reality check and saved by the third party.

"I'll be right back."

"She's almost done." Lizzie gestured at Reena sniffing nearby.

Kelan exited the car and Walker greeted him.

"Dude, you'll do anything to get out of working the manhunt, huh?" Kelan teased.

"Believe me, I'd rather have trudged through the mountains." Walker chuckled. "Any progress on the escapees?"

"No, and I'm beat." Kelan sighed. "It's no small feat to climb through the wilderness in search of criminals." He withdrew a large pizza box from the passenger seat, passing it to Walker.

"That smells amazing. We appreciate this." Lizzie and Reena joined them, and they headed inside.

"Best in town, or so I'm told," Kelan replied.

The group dived into the meal, scarcely speaking. By the time they'd finished, Walker felt like he'd fallen into a carb coma. "That was exceptional."

"Great choice," Lizzie commended.

Kelan leaned back on the sofa, with his arms behind his head. "It was the least I could do for you allowing me to crash here while we work the manhunt."

"All LEO hands on deck is a good thing," Walker said.

"One hundred percent," Lizzie replied.

"Any details on the search today?" Walker asked.

"Not much. Same story." Kelan exhaled a long breath. "Oh, there was a little drama at the command post when Sierra Boyer, the sister of one of the corrections officers, Miller Boyer, came in demanding to know if it was his body on the prison bus." Kelan shook his head. "Poor girl's a mess. They're pretty certain Miller is one of the deceased guards. Although the manifest included him, positive identification awaits DNA comparison with Sierra because of his extensive injuries."

Lizzie hung her head. "How sad. I can't imagine the pain of wondering and hoping that it's not your sibling."

"Yeah."

"Doesn't he have DNA in the system since he's a guard?" Lizzie asked.

"Should have," Walker replied. "But testing isn't overnight."

"Right," Lizzie said.

The group talked about the case and sharing work stories until the sun had set.

Kelan yawned. "Sorry, I'm terrible company."

"No, we're all beat," Lizzie said.

"Walker, I'll take the sofa tonight. You can have Lizzie's bed."

She shook her head. "Captain Cole got a glass repairman here while we were battling the shooter in the woods."

"Excellent. Get some rest," Kelan said. "I'm good with taking tonight's couch watch."

Walker yawned. "Don't have to ask me twice." He got to his feet and bid the other two goodnight. Kelan's arrival had kept him from making a huge mistake. What was he thinking? He couldn't ask Lizzie about dating. The exhaustion had caused his reasoning to go wonky. Walker's life revolved around work. His job wouldn't let him down or have unreasonable expectations of him. He'd fought that battle once four years ago with JoLynn, and she'd abruptly ended it. She'd never understood the responsibilities he bore or that he didn't work a nine-to-five schedule. Their relationship had been doomed from the start, but that didn't make the hurt any less.

He headed to the spare bedroom, leaving the door cracked in case they needed more than one set of ears.

Resolved in the decision, Walker replaced his emotional guard and focused on the motive someone had for putting them on a kill list. Despite his best efforts, his mind lingered on Lizzie.

He closed his eyes, desperate to ignore his heart's longing for a second chance with her.

* * *

Lizzie startled and nearly dropped her coffee mug when her phone rang. She'd scarcely taken a sip, still half-asleep, before the call reminded her about the COK9 team meeting. She bounded from the kitchen to her bedroom and unplugged the device from the charger, glimpsing the screen. Lizzie winced, answering on the third ring. "Morning," she croaked.

"Hey, Lizzie," tech analyst Eva Gomez greeted her. "Hold on while everyone else connects."

At least Lizzie had taken a shower earlier and looked presentable, even if her brain wasn't firing on all cylinders. She settled onto her bed, leaning against the headboard, as a series of clicks preceded the other task force members joining the call. Eva, Trevor Slate and FBI Supervisory Special Agent Emmett Dane appeared on the screen, sitting on one side of the headquarters conference table. Colorado Springs officer Maren Anderson and Eli Blackwood from Oak City PD sat opposite them. Canyon Creek officer Autumn Riley joined via video, followed by Melody Rust from Boulder PD and River Jameson from Ridge PD.

Thoughts of Walker had kept Lizzie tossing and turning. The previous day's events and the late-night chat with Kelan and Walker had tipped her off her game. Especially when she'd flat out asked Walker about Presley and he'd clammed up. Even after all these years, he refused to own his side. The response reminded her of how hurt she'd felt after all the ways Zeke had found to deceive her. Was Walker cut from the same protect-thyself-at-any-cost cloth? Zeke had had no problem tossing her under the proverbial bus to save himself. *Get a grip, Lizzie.* Those two things weren't even connected. Zeke's bad shoot was a far cry from Walker's teenage antics. Yet the emotional wound remained. Evasiveness, lies—it all had the same root. Regardless, there was no room for the romantic nonsense when she had two big cases to solve.

"Thanks everyone for joining in early today," Emmett said. "Can you all hear me?"

A round of "affirmative," "yes" and "go ahead" filled the line.

Lizzie glanced out the window, where periwinkle, rose, and cerulean colored the sunrise. Walker and Kelan were working in the living room, leaving her alone in her bedroom for the next hour.

"Great," Emmett said. "I'll step back and ask Eva to please take the lead and update the group."

"Thanks to Lizzie and Trevor's interrogation of Benny Fuller, I ran the alias 'Trigger' through the system," Eva said. "However, it didn't produce any hits. Additionally, it appears informants won't talk about him, which eliminates any leads on identifying him."

"That speaks to Trigger's reputation, and the danger associated with him," Emmett added.

"I have an informant with a pulse on the underground creeps hiding in the shadows," Lizzie offered. "I'll reach out to him and see if he'll talk."

"If other criminals aren't willing to give up Trigger, why would he?" Trevor asked.

"It's worth a try," Lizzie said. "He's always willing to assist us when there's the possibility of a big payout."

"I agree," Emmett replied. "Thank you, Lizzie. Please follow up with him. Once he names his price for a lead on Trigger, I'll see what I can do."

"Roger that."

They concluded the group meeting and Lizzie returned to the kitchen to warm her coffee in the microwave, then started for the living room. Walker's and Kelan's voices carried through the open window. She spotted them sitting on the front porch with their backs to her.

Reena got up from her dog bed, stretching and yawning simultaneously. Lizzie had just reached for the front door when Kelan's next words froze her in place. "I didn't put it together that your Lizzie is the former Littleton PD officer involved in that shooting until last night."

Her heart drummed, and she leaned closer, staying hidden behind the curtain to eavesdrop.

"I don't know what you're talking about," Walker said.

"I've got a few friends at LPD, so this is secondhand knowledge. She and another officer were working on a robbery three years ago and one of the suspects was shot and killed."

"That's awful, but sadly not unusual these days."

"Right, but there was a lot of hoopla with it."

Memories from that night flooded Lizzie from all directions. Zeke had pulled the trigger, killing the suspect. But Lizzie had told the truth, which sent her packing along with him.

She listened as Kalen conveyed the story to Walker. Unable to participate as a silent observer anymore, she tugged open the door and released Reena.

Both men twisted to face her with guilt-ridden expressions.

"That's mostly correct," she said, leaning against the railing.

Reena retrieved the ball and dropped it at Walker's feet. He smiled and tossed the toy for her.

"My bad. I only remember what my friends shared," Kelan said sheepishly. He lifted his phone. "Oh, I missed a call, excuse me." He scurried inside.

Walker shrugged uncomfortably. "We didn't mean to talk about you behind your back."

"It's public information, so it's no secret," Lizzie replied.

"You don't have to tell me anything."

"And what? Leave you believing a lie?" Lizzie studied Walker, trying to decide whether to share the story. She sighed and slid into the chair beside him. "Kelan was right. It happened three years ago, and it was the perfect storm. Everything that could go wrong did. Zeke and I were both employed at Littleton PD, and we responded to a call for a robbery in progress. We were also dating at the time."

"Were you partnered?"

"No, that was against policy, but we worked the same shift." She stared out, avoiding Walker's gaze. "I arrived and was approaching the store when I heard a gunshot. I hesitated, assured backup was en route. The radio call didn't provide details regarding the number of parties inside the store. Zeke was a glory hog and wanted the attention of a big takedown, so he'd gone in, guns blazing, before reinforcement arrived. I had to cover him—"

"He didn't give you a choice," Walker defended.

She appreciated the effort, but she'd faced her mistakes a long time ago. "I inched around the door and saw Zeke placing a gun in the hands of an unconscious female suspect on the floor. And before you ask, no, my body camera didn't capture it, because I peeked around the corner."

"Your body camera was hidden by the door," Walker surmised.

"Right. After backup arrived and we took the perps into custody, I learned the deceased woman was Jennifer Mace, who worked at the store. She'd helped stage a robbery, permitting her husband, Otho Mace, and son, Eddie Waterhouse, to 'rob' the place while she was on duty. Both heard the shot, which was why they claimed to have returned fire, unaware until the end that Jennifer was deceased."

"Wow."

"Zeke begged me not to tell the chief about him placing the gun in Jennifer's hands. He insisted she'd rammed the door into him, causing his body camera to fall off. Footage confirmed that, because it dies when it hits the concrete. Zeke claimed he shot Jennifer in self-defense, and she dropped the gun. He feared Internal Affairs would make a big deal about it and he'd lose his job. Since his body camera didn't capture the shooting, there was no proof."

"What did you do?"

"As soon as Zeke started making excuses, I realized the shoot was bad and he was covering himself. Zeke said if I loved him, I wouldn't tell, then threatened to break up with me and ruin my career if I did."

Walker worked his jaw but didn't reply.

"Though I had no body camera footage to prove my story, I went to the chief anyway. Thankfully, he believed me and offered Zeke the chance to resign instead of being publicly fired."

"I'm sorry you had to deal with that." Walker shook his head.

Reena rushed to them, carrying her ball.

Lizzie reached down and took the toy, tossing it into the yard again. "I returned to Bison Valley after Zeke was fired, which basically destroyed his law enforcement career. I haven't heard from him since."

Lizzie blew out a long breath. "Our fellow officers sided with Zeke, accusing me of crossing the line and not backing him. I became a pariah. It was his word against mine. I moved home with my commanding officer's full praising referral. They couldn't prove either of us had told the truth."

Walker threw the ball again to Reena, and they sat in silence for several minutes.

She looked down at her feet.

"The brotherhood—it's great when you're part of it. But I've seen it turn on its own before."

"Yeah, they can really ostracize anyone they feel doesn't belong," Lizzie concluded.

She didn't expect absolution, but the simple sentence helped her to at least make eye contact with him. "The entire experience taught me a lot. Ultimately, I'm glad I returned to Bison Valley. I enjoy working and serving the community where we grew up."

"Thank you for telling me," Walker said. The kindness in his expression warmed her heart. She saw no condemnation there, only understanding.

Kelan exited the house. "Hey, sorry, but I've gotta run to

the command center. Is there anything you need from me before I go?"

"No, I don't think so," Walker replied.

"I forgot my phone charger, could I borrow yours this morning?" Kelan asked.

"Sure, I'll grab it for you." Walker rushed back into the house.

"Lizzie, I'm really sorry about earlier," Kelan said. "I should've clarified with you before I spoke." He placed a hand on her shoulder, offering a gentle squeeze.

"Trust but verify," Lizzie teased.

"Precisely." He smiled. "But I had no business sticking my size-eleven boot into my big mouth."

She chuckled. "It's all good. We know how the law enforcement gossip mill runs."

Kelan winced. "My bad for contributing to it today. For what it's worth, you didn't deserve the LPD backlash."

Lizzie offered Kelan a nod and bit her quivering lip. The screen door slapped shut and Walker handed Kelan the car charger.

"Appreciate it," Kelan said. "I'll catch you all at the manhunt." He offered a last wave, then headed for his SUV.

"Everything okay?" Walker asked.

The question caused the dam on her emotions to erupt, and tears streamed down her cheeks. How long had it been since someone asked if she was okay after the Zeke nightmare?

Walker pulled her into a hug. "Sometimes you gotta let those tears out," he whispered.

Once she'd collected herself again, Lizzie withdrew from Walker's touch. "I don't normally get upset like that."

"I'm guessing it was a long time in coming." Walker smiled.

"How'd you get so sensitive?"

"Natural talent," he quipped.

"Your girlfriend's blessed to have you." Lizzie let the comment hang between them.

"I'm not involved with anyone."

She tried to hide the relief in her tone. "I suppose having a relationship is hard with your job."

"Significant others don't adjust well to the marshal schedule." A look passed over Walker's face that Lizzie couldn't quite describe.

"Makes sense. Even with another law enforcement officer, I could see that being a challenge."

"I'm starving."

Lizzie took the brisk shift as the end of the discussion. "Breakfast sounds good." She whistled for Reena. "Give me a second. I need to reach out to my CI." She hurried inside and grabbed her cell, dialing the informant's number, but it rang through to voice mail. Hopefully the name Trigger would be familiar to him. "Hey, Dex, it's Lizzie. Call me ASAP." He normally returned her calls right away, especially if there was financial gain for him.

Though it wasn't reasonable, she remembered how caring and kind Walker had been. That man still existed beneath the muscles and badge. Against her mind's argument and the circling doubts she presented in return, the old crush she'd had on Walker had returned full force. But, she reminded herself, her failed relationship with Zeke and the fallout on her career afterward had taught her it was unwise to get involved with another LEO. She'd thought working in the same career, even the same agency, would be beneficial, but the intertwining of her career and her personal life had been a disaster after the shooting. Though she and Walker didn't serve the same agency, it didn't matter. She'd not allow herself to fall for Walker McCane, either.

He'd already broken her heart once.

No. She'd never make that foolish choice again.

She paused, taking one last glance out toward her property. And until she found whoever was trying to abduct her and, more importantly, figured out why they wanted her, she couldn't afford distractions.

Not even a stunning deputy US marshal with a gentle heart and drop-dead-gorgeous looks. But being held in Walker's arms had awakened parts of Lizzie's heart she'd thought were dead. For the first time since Zeke's betrayal, Lizzie wondered if her vow to stay single was justified. Then, just as memories of Zeke often did, Lizzie remembered how her fellow officers had turned on her, taking Zeke's side. The loneliness and sorrow she'd experienced had devastated her. She didn't have the energy to reinvent herself again if everything went wrong with Walker. Surely, he'd not do what Zeke had done, but he wasn't in a relationship, either. Why? She glanced out the window, to where Walker played with Reena. They'd known each other since high school. Just like she and Zeke. But that was a long time ago. She'd been wrong about Zeke. What did she really know about Walker McCane? She headed outside to join him, and he faced her with concern in his expression. "Hey, I've been thinking about what you said."

"I said a lot of things."

"What if Otho Mace put you on the kill list? You were there the night his wife died."

"But Zeke was the one who shot her," Lizzie defended. "Although rationality isn't something criminals are known for."

"Right."

Lizzie blinked. "I hadn't considered that. And if he'd sent Eddie to do it—"

"And he died in the prison bus crash."

"—he'd have another reason to want me dead," Lizzie concluded.

SIX

Walker spent the morning searching, in vain, for Zeke's social media accounts. Apparently, that wasn't something the man invested his time using. The only online result produced a brief news story focused on the liquor store shooting.

The conversation with Lizzie had left him in deep contemplations. She'd done the right thing and faced unfair repercussions. Fury that Zeke hadn't protected Lizzie and instead had blamed and turned others against her raged through Walker. True, he hated injustice, but there was more to his emotions.

He still cared for Lizzie.

Not an option, Walker. He ran his hand through his hair in a futile effort to suppress his out-of-control thoughts. He resolved to keep his interactions with Lizzie focused on the case and nothing more. Yet, he'd not deny that even with that in mind, the threats to her safety and the protective instincts that coursed through him had awakened Walker's feelings for her.

Lizzie's account of the shooting incident hadn't surprised Walker in the slightest. None of Zeke's illegal and immoral requests for Lizzie to hide the truth were out of character for him. Rather, it confirmed everything Walker had learned after parting from their toxic friendship. Zeke would steal from stores and call it fun. He'd seen Zeke's selfish drive to get what he wanted and couldn't afford. Zeke had cheated on school exams, then lied when he got caught. Zeke also enjoyed keeping Walker down with verbal insults while boosting himself higher with claims to be joking. And he'd deserted Walker after winning Lizzie's affections, knowing full well how much Walker liked her. It had taken too long for Walker to realize Zeke was no friend.

Walker returned his thoughts to the case. Had Otho Mace ordered the attack on Lizzie?

"Hey, Walker, we're ready when you are," Lizzie called, interrupting his thoughts.

"Coming." He slid his laptop into his backpack and left the spare room. "Let's roll." He offered what he hoped was a convincing smile that played off his disappointment and hid his endless racing thoughts.

She loaded Reena into the kennel, and they climbed into her SUV. Neither said much as they exited her property and headed for the command center.

Questions about Zeke lingered on the tip of Walker's tongue, and his only hesitancy was the awareness that he'd no right to inquire in her personal life. Had she not overheard the conversation with Kelan, she probably wouldn't have shared the details.

"Have you asked your dad about the remaining escapees?" she asked.

Walker shook off his contemplations, mentally smacking himself for not doing that before she'd reminded him. "Actually, I'll call him now." His father answered on the first ring. "Hey, Dad."

"I'm glad you called. I'm going a little stir-crazy being cooped up here."

"No issues, though?"

"None. Just a case of boredom."

"I'm sorry." His father hated sitting still. "Hopefully it won't be much longer," Walker encouraged. "We're working hard to close this case."

"I have complete confidence in you, son."

"While I've got you on the phone, do the names Gregory Juhl, Anthony Arnold, Otho Mace, Eddie Waterhouse or Vance Herrera mean anything to you?"

His father paused, then replied, "No, why?"

"They're persons of interest in the prison escape."

"And you think one of them put us on this kill list?"

"Possibly."

"I haven't a clue."

"I'll keep in touch, but please be careful." Walker disconnected and addressed Lizzie. "He doesn't recognize them."

Lizzie sighed. "That would've been too easy."

"No kidding." Walker rolled down the window, permitting fresh air to enter the cab.

"I have a call in to Captain Cole to find out where Otho Mace is now. He'll call back when he has intel."

"I think that'll answer a lot of questions," Walker said.

"It's a reasonable motive to kill me, but why you and your father?"

Walker frowned. "That part I haven't figured out yet."

Several miles passed in silence before Walker said, "I admit the past few attacks have me concerned about whether we might be in over our heads. Especially if there's more than one perpetrator." What he didn't add was his fear about protecting her from several criminals cooperating on a kill list. More importantly, how was he supposed to guard his emotions? No matter how many times he reasoned out all the things that didn't work between them, his stubborn heart continued to hope.

"We've held our own against the attacks. And you've done a stellar job. Besides, I'm a skilled cop, remember?" Teasing hung in her question, but it didn't alleviate Walker's apprehensions.

She parked in an open spot near the command post, and he waited as she unloaded Reena. They approached the unit and nearly collided with a blonde woman exiting simultaneously. Tears streaked her face. "Excuse me." She rushed past them, leaving Walker and Lizzie confused.

They met Captain Cole inside, and he wore a perplexed expression.

"Sir?" Lizzie asked.

"Sometimes this is the hardest job in the world," he mumbled.

"Please collect the search grid map and resume your search." He turned away, not giving them further explanation.

Lizzie shrugged at Walker's inquisitive frown.

He gathered the information, and she held up a finger, motioning toward Captain Cole to indicate she planned to talk to her boss. "Would you take Reena for a second?"

Walker nodded and accepted the leash, heading outside with Reena.

He watched as the other searchers started into the wilderness and hoped today would be the day they'd capture the remaining convicts.

Lizzie exited the command post and rushed to him. "Captain Cole met with Sierra Boyer when we arrived."

"The woman who just walked out bawling?" Walker clarified.

"Yep. She's the sister of Miller Boyer, who they have confirmed is one of the deceased prison guards."

"I remember. That's too bad. I dreaded giving death notifications," Walker passed Reena's leash to Lizzie.

"Me, too."

"But at least she has closure," Walker said.

The sobering discussion shifted his focus, rightfully so, onto the task at hand.

They traveled to Raspberry Butte and continued their quest through the forest. Only the sound of their footsteps crunching on the pine needles, dead leaves and branches filled the space between them. Even the radios were silent, indicating the others weren't locating leads or trails, either. The more time that passed, the less chance they had of finding the men.

The steep incline and rocky path made the trek difficult. After hiking for several hours, they paused for a break. Lizzie handed him a granola bar and a bottle of water.

"Thanks."

He stared at her, wondering what would've happened if their

prom night hadn't gone so horribly wrong. Or if he'd tried harder to defend himself.

"Why are you looking at me like that?" She took a sip of water.

"I was thinking about high school." The words escaped his lips before he stopped them.

"Really? About what?"

He glanced down. No turning back now. "I had a huge crush on you."

"Yeah, right." Lizzie dismissed him with a wave of her hand.

"No, it's true," Walker said.

Lizzie blinked and tilted her head. "So why did you kiss Presley Quintana for all to see?"

Walker heard the defensiveness in her tone.

Ouch. "If I told you that kiss wasn't what it seemed, you'd say my reasoning sounded weak, even though it's the truth."

"I'm all ears."

"Promise you won't hurl any sharp objects at me?"

Lizzie laughed and glanced around. "There's an abundance of rocks, but I assure you, I can handle honest confessions."

"How far back do you want me to go?"

"Um, I guess as far as necessary?" She sat atop a boulder, legs dangling.

Walker cleared his throat, offered a prayer of courage, then said, "I told you my mom left my dad and me. They divorced my junior year of high school."

Compassion shadowed her face. "What a terrible time for you to endure that. I'm sorry, I didn't know."

"Thanks. It was rough."

Walker glanced down, studying the stone's intricate pattern. "Guess my mom got tired of us."

Empathy swarmed Lizzie's eyes and Walker forced himself to avert his gaze. "Anyway, that was the start of my insecurities."

"Walker McCane, insecure?" She frowned, disbelieving. "Not possible."

"I assure you, my mom did a number on my self-esteem. If she didn't want me, why would anyone else?"

Lizzie tilted her head. "Walker, surely you understand that's a lie."

"Maybe." Walker paused. "I don't want to waste your time talking about my history."

"I'm intrigued. Spill."

"Zeke told me he'd overheard you talking to one of your friends about how you wanted him to ask you to prom instead of me—"

"Whoa, he said what?" Lizzie bolted off the boulder. "That did. Not. Happen." She punctuated each word.

Stunned, Walker blinked, unsure how to proceed. Was she covering her embarrassment at getting caught? "I understood. Zeke was the charismatic, fun one. I got over it, but for the rest of what I'm about to share, I had to start with that foundation."

"Sorry, I'll refrain from interrupting. But when you're finished, we will clarify misconceptions."

"All righty." He exhaled. "I was mega nervous about asking you out. Truly, I was shocked when you agreed."

"I had a huge crush on *you*, so it was a no-brainer."

Walker considered her words. "You did?"

"Um, yeah."

"But—" Walker swallowed. "Sorry, I'm trying to piece this all together."

"Tell me your version, then we can deal with Zeke's lies," Lizzie replied.

"It took me all junior and senior year to get up the courage to ask you out. Prom was the now-or-never option. But that night, at the dance, Zeke told me about the conversation between you and your friend—"

"Which never happened." She lifted her hand. "Sorry, go ahead."

"Zeke acted like he was offended for me and claimed he hadn't wanted to tell me about it, but he also didn't want you to use me."

Lizzie's jaw visibly tightened.

Walker withheld that he'd been devastated, and it had fueled his insecurities about dating Lizzie. The next part would only exacerbate his pathetic story. "It wasn't until the next week that I discovered Zeke paid Presley to kiss me in front of you. He ensured you'd see it and hate me."

"What a jerk." Lizzie crushed her empty water bottle. "He planned it so he could make his move."

It did appear that way, but Walker refrained from saying the words.

"I'd be stunned except after years of doing life with Zeke, I understand his MO."

"He absolutely had a modus operandi," Walker added.

"Oh, yeah. Zeke's a master manipulator."

"Truth is, I thought you were out of my league."

"Me? Why?" Walker stared in disbelief.

"Every girl at school was crushing on you."

"You're delusional." Walker chuckled. "Maybe drink more water."

She swatted playfully at him. "It's true. You seriously didn't know? Why do you think Zeke had to manipulate his way around you? He was jealous."

Walker considered her words. "I never knew." Memories of Zeke's harsh jokes and degrading comments bounced to mind.

"Don't beat yourself up for not seeing it. I learned the hard way that Zeke was a chameleon of deception."

Walker stepped closer and gently took her hand. "Lizzie, I'm truly sorry for all that happened at prom. If I could do it again, I'd have fought harder for you."

She glanced down, but she didn't withdraw from his touch. "I wish you had." Her long eyelashes shadowed her beautiful emerald eyes.

His gaze traveled the contour of her face to her lips. *No. Off-limits. Career first.* Walker stepped back, releasing his hold.

"Why didn't you tell me the truth?" Hurt lingered in her voice.

Walker shot her a raised eyebrow. "Hard to do when you refused to speak to me."

Lizzie winced. "Fair enough."

The radio chirped with an update from another team stating they were relocating.

"We should keep moving," Walker said.

"Right." Lizzie gathered Reena's collapsible bowl and tucked it into her backpack, and they continued. "Zeke played up the situation and claimed he'd defended me."

This time Walker snorted. "After talking to Presley, Zeke and I had it out." Memories of the argument and subsequent falling-out still grated on Walker. The *should've, could've* things he'd failed to address. "I left for college shortly thereafter. Besides, when I returned to Colorado and learned through the Bison Valley grapevine that you two were an item, I figured it had all played out as it was supposed to."

She walked ahead of him, talking over her shoulder. "I don't even know what to say. I'm sorry, Walker. If I'd given you a chance to explain, things might've turned out differently."

"Yeah, funny how Zeke made sure to keep us apart."

"Of course, he rushed in like a knight in shining armor. That night, he drove me home, and I cried on his shoulder. He encouraged me to steer clear of you, saying you'd lie and manipulate the conversation."

Anger boiled within Walker. "How did we let ten years pass without dealing with all this?"

"If I didn't know him better, I wouldn't believe it, but after the shooting, none of this surprises me," Lizzie said.

Walker had no doubts Lizzie's version of the incident was the truth.

They paused at a split in the path. "Hmm, which way?" Walker asked, pulling out the map.

She leaned closer to him, studying the diagram. Lizzie lifted her face, meeting his gaze. They stood, staring at one another. The rays of the summer sun pierced the canopy of leaves. Bird-songs filling the atmosphere. The unbearable need to hold her had Walker reaching out to touch her cheek. Her soft skin beneath his fingertips was like an electric shock. She closed her eyes.

Walker leaned in.

And his phone rang.

He jerked back and glanced at the screen, spotting Vandeaux's name. "I've gotta take this."

Lizzie smiled, diverting her attention to Reena as Walker swiped to answer. "Hey, boss."

"We've got an update. Authorities found the body of escapee Nolan Trusty outside of Denver. Apparently, he tried carjacking the wrong guy's pickup. The man fought back and won."

"Excellent."

Lizzie watched him with interest.

"And good news, two others, Hayden Aryan and Ira Jose, were apprehended at the bus station, attempting to flee town on their handsome looks." Vandeaux snorted. "I love dumb criminals."

"Absolutely." Walker chuckled. "Are either of them talking about the ambush?"

"Negative."

"I figured that'd be too easy. So, we're down to the last three escapees."

"Yes," Vandeaux replied. "Gregory Juhl, Anthony Arnold and Vance Herrera."

"Well, that narrows it down for us, too. Juhl would have cause to come after me. It's possible my father is merely collateral damage."

"It's not inconceivable," Vandeaux agreed.

"But that doesn't compute with Lizzie. Juhl wouldn't know her, and she doesn't know Arnold or Herrera."

"We'll keep digging into their backgrounds but be vigilant. They haven't given up yet, and short of you two going into protective custody with your dad, I'm not sure what else we can do at this point."

Walker glanced at Lizzie, pressing the phone tight against his ear to prevent her from overhearing the comment. "I'll offer that option." Walker shared the information about the shooting and the connection with Otho Mace. "Captain Cole is working on finding out where Mace is now."

"Good work. Let me know if I need to jump in. Keep in touch."

They disconnected, and Lizzie rose from where she'd knelt beside Reena.

Walker updated her. "Vandeaux suggested—"

"No way," Lizzie interrupted. "Don't even try the protective-custody card. It's not happening."

"I figured you'd say that."

"Let's think beyond the obvious and omit Mace for now. Why wouldn't Juhl come after me to hurt you?"

"It's not unheard-of. But they don't know our history. Why not go after Captain Cole?"

"Good point."

"Let's find these criminals before they strike again."

"Yes." Lizzie gestured toward the break in the path. "Let's see what Reena thinks." She offered the scent articles once more to Reena and ordered, "Find."

The dog sniffed the items, then the trail, repeating the move before she aimed for the right.

"Guess this way," Lizzie said.

Walker fell in step behind the team, grateful Vandeaux had called when he did. He'd saved Walker from making the worst possible mistake. What was he thinking? He'd nearly kissed

Lizzie. No, that was unacceptable. *Focus, McCane.* They were running out of time, and he had confused his priorities.

Job one, find the convicts.

Two, steer clear of Lizzie Reynolds.

Lizzie jolted awake from the recurring nightmare she'd thought had finally gone away. Like the rerun of a bad movie, Jennifer Mace professed her innocence. Lizzie bent down to help her, and Jennifer reached for the gun hidden in her back pocket and aimed it at Lizzie. She always woke up before Jennifer fired her weapon. The scene resuscitated questions that had plagued Lizzie for years. She'd not realized how retelling the entire story to Walker would impact her psyche. But the discussion had apparently activated all those horrible memories and brought them to the surface.

Suppressing the thoughts, Lizzie rolled to her side with a groan. Every muscle in her body ached after the long days of hiking the tough mountain terrain, along with fleeing a kidnapper. The strenuous physical exertion surpassed all her CrossFit workouts. The added frustration of not finding the convicts also wore her out. She'd not complained to Walker, though, since it would only contribute to his nagging advice for Lizzie to go into protective detail. She'd finish these cases if it killed her.

Reena snored softly at Lizzie's feet. The clock on her nightstand beamed 4:20 in blue LED numbers. She stretched for the curtain, wincing at the soreness still present in her ribs. The morning chirping of birds carried through the closed window. Lizzie lay on her back, staring at the whirring ceiling fan above her in the dark bedroom. She was in no hurry to get out of her comfortable bed.

She and Walker had returned to her house exhausted the night before and agreed to crash early. She'd not seen Kelan since yesterday. Reena hadn't alerted if he'd returned in the night. He'd either chosen to stay somewhere else, or her faithful companion had grown accustomed to his presence. Lizzie grinned at the sleeping canine.

Her thoughts traveled to Walker. Neither had brought up the awkward almost-kiss, but based on the way it had stilted their conversation the rest of the day, it had apparently affected Walker as much as it had Lizzie. Had he regretted the action? Half of her wished they'd followed through. She couldn't deny the attraction she felt for him. But the reasonable side of Lizzie warned she had a job to do. Besides, a man had once nearly cost Lizzie her career. Not that Walker was that kind of person. Still, there was no time or place for such nonsense now.

The sobering reminder had Lizzie considering the escaped convicts again, and she sought the connection to her, apart from revenge against Walker. She had nothing in common with the criminals. She'd not arrested them or worked on cases involving them. But until they had Otho Mace's status, he remained the most viable connection.

An idea bounced to mind. Was Dex, her confidential informant, associated with them? No, that did not compute. Why would he want to eliminate the income from helping law enforcement? Still, he'd not returned her call, which was unusual. Lizzie made a mental note to try contacting him again later in the morning.

Only Eddie Waterhouse—Jennifer Mace's son—had a direct link to Lizzie. But he'd died in the ambush. Unless he had a friend with a serious loyalty promise to eliminate Lizzie, she couldn't explain why someone was targeting her. And that didn't make sense considering the kill list included Mr. McCane and Walker.

It seemed more likely Gregory Juhl had targeted Walker as revenge. If he intended to inflict as much damage and pain as possible, it stood to reason that he'd go after Mr. McCane.

Except why come for Lizzie? After the multiple kidnapping attempts, they knew whoever it was wanted Lizzie alive. Yet, she and Walker were nothing more than coworkers, and they'd not reunited until after the first attack. With her mind circling the same annoying track, Lizzie shoved off the covers, giving up on going back to sleep.

At her movement, Reena lifted her head and offered Lizzie a lazy gaze.

"Sorry, girl, I know it's early." She ruffled the dog's velvety fur.

Reena yawned, emitting a squeak, and stretched out all four paws. She didn't rise. Instead, she lay staring at Lizzie as though pleading for a little more time.

"Okay, you win." Lizzie chuckled. "I'll take a shower while you finish resting."

Another yawn and Reena closed her eyes.

She headed for the bathroom, and when she'd finished getting ready, Lizzie returned to her bedroom, where Reena sat patiently by the door. A clear indicator she needed to go outside. "C'mon, sleepyhead, but we need to be quiet, so we don't wake the others."

Reena offered a dramatic sigh and gave a thorough shake.

With a hand signal for Reena to be quiet, Lizzie opened the door, and they ventured into the hallway with the staccato clicking of the dog's nails on the floor. She glanced in the direction of the living room, but the person there was covered by a blanket, face hidden from view. Kelan and Walker had chosen their sleeping arrangements. Lizzie had gone to bed, uninterested in the outcome.

They moved through the kitchen and exited through the back door. Lizzie closed the door gently behind her. She allowed Reena to walk off leash while keeping her dog in view.

The moon was full and hovered low, casting ambient light over her property. The older acreage needed a little TLC, but it had great potential. Lizzie envisioned all the things she'd do to improve her home. The best part of her land butted against the foothills, which gradually rose into the breathtaking mountain backdrop and spiky tree line. Thick evergreens and scattered boulders dotted the earth, creating a picturesque scene. She loved this place, and until the kidnapping attempt, she'd always felt safe. Would that security return?

Lost in her thoughts, Lizzie startled when Kelan appeared from the shadows. She covered her mouth, stifling the scream that threatened to escape. She rested her hand over her chest, ribs still tender, and heaved relief. "You nearly gave me a heart attack."

"Sorry about that." Kelan winced. "I heard movement and came out to check." He seemed to study her. "You're going to catch a cold standing here in flip-flops and a short-sleeved T-shirt."

She glanced down. "My joggers are warm, though," she countered.

Kelan chuckled. "Okay…"

"Didn't think anyone was awake."

Kelan paused, glancing at Reena sniffing the ground beside her. "You two are up early."

"Couldn't sleep," she countered. "What're you doing out here already? I thought you were still asleep."

"I need to meet with the DA before court today." Kelan sighed. "The fun never ends with marshal duties."

"I hear you. I'm working the illegal adoption ring case," Lizzie said.

"Any leads?" Kelan tugged his backpack higher on his shoulder.

"No, but I'm hoping once I finally get ahold of my CI, that'll change."

"Chasing down CIs will keep you on your toes." Kelan laughed.

"Absolutely," Lizzie smiled. "We'll have to compare stories sometime."

"Anytime. I still owe you for letting me stay here."

"No, you don't." Lizzie meant it. She'd enjoyed getting to

know Kelan and having him and Walker around was a measure of comfort after all the bizarre things that had happened. But that wouldn't last forever, and she'd not allow herself to become reliant on them.

Reena returned and nudged Kelan's hand. "Hey, beautiful." He ruffled her fur, and she relished the touch. "Wish I could stick around but I have to get on the road before rush hour. I'll go wake Walker."

"No, let him sleep. Reena shouldn't be much longer, and we'll go inside as soon she's done. Besides, the patrol unit is still parked down there." She pointed toward the driveway where the vehicle sat.

Kelan gave a skeptical frown. "Are you sure?"

"Positive."

"As long as you promise to go inside as soon as Reena is finished doing her business."

"Promise," Lizzie replied, glancing at her dog still wandering the yard. "She's got a ritual of ensuring the space meets her standards."

Kelan grinned. "See ya later."

They parted company and Lizzie watched as Kelan rounded the house then disappeared. A few seconds later, the beam of his headlights stretched out onto the road as he drove away. Just because she couldn't sleep didn't mean she'd take that away from Walker. They'd all worked long hours, and the hikes through the Colorado wilderness were brutal. Maybe she'd whip up breakfast for them. Lizzie's mind wandered. What did Walker like to eat?

Her thoughts traveled to their high school years, the easy conversations they'd shared since reuniting, and back to the almost-kiss.

Lizzie watched Reena sniffing along the line of evergreens. The moonlight and start of the sunrise provided enough illumination to see where she was going while maintaining the darkened haze.

Her thoughts bounced to Mia Andrews and the three murdered teens. Mia was the team's lifeline to finding the killer, because unlike the other teens, she had loving grandparents. The Andrewses had raised Mia the past five years after her parents' deaths, and they refused to give up on her. Additionally, Mia didn't fit the victimology. She had no need to run away, since her grandparents had promised their full support throughout her pregnancy as well as assistance in raising her baby.

The baby's father had nervously cooperated with the investigation thus far. Lizzie snorted. Although he'd admitted to dumping Mia when she told him about the pregnancy. Jerk.

Regardless, Mia had COK9 searching tirelessly for her. Lizzie's mental traversing shifted to the missing convicts and the fatal shooting, then boomeranged to Walker. Of all the other options, he was a pleasant place to park her harried mind for a little while, so she permitted herself a few moments to indulge.

The time with him had surprised Lizzie, and she was grateful they'd talked through all the misconceptions. The anger she felt for Zeke and his lies inspired Lizzie to increase her pace as Reena got closer to the edge of the yard.

The handsome, wonderful guy she'd crushed hard on in high school—once a tall, thin athlete—had grown into a muscular, drop-dead gorgeous deputy US marshal with a kind and generous personality. Why couldn't he be a jerk? He'd be so much easier to resist.

Their discussion and the reminder of what happened with Zeke presented Lizzie an important and essential wake-up call, but her resolve had weakened slightly. She'd vowed to never get romantically involved with another LEO, but Walker was making her reconsider.

Zeke's lies seemed endless. He'd claimed Walker abandoned their friendship after Zeke confronted him about Lizzie. Her knight in shining armor was nothing more than a snake in disguise. He'd justified his nefarious actions. And of course he'd chosen Presley Quintana in the ruse, considering she hated Lizzie. Knowing Presley, she'd have kissed Walker for free.

After all these years, she had finally learned the truth about Zeke's part in the devastation of her prom night. The realization that he'd played her since high school frustrated Lizzie. She'd fallen for his protector-boyfriend act. What a fool.

She skidded to a halt, processing the revelation. If she'd failed to see the truth in Zeke, how could she trust herself to choose a healthy relationship? She'd known Zeke and Walker from a young age, and yet, she'd believed Zeke's fabrication. Relationships and Lizzie were not a good combination.

Just another reason Walker McCane was 100 percent off-limits.

She glanced up, but Reena was nowhere in sight. How long had she been daydreaming? "Reena?"

Lizzie's pulse increased. "Reena."

Her retriever was laser focused while tracking, but she was off leash now. The dog wasn't oblivious to basic canine instincts like chasing rabbits and deer who dared to cross her path. Lizzie sprinted toward the tree line, entering the forest. The hairs rose on her arms and neck in visceral response, and she visually roved the area. She hugged herself to ward off the chill.

"Reena?" Her voice quivered and she chided herself. This was her property. She had no reason to fear, and she was safe. Reena would alert to any strangers. Except her dog was nowhere to be found.

Lizzie struggled to move fast in her flip-flops. The thin plastic wasn't a strong barrier from the pine needles that littered the ground. A cool breeze sent a shiver up her back, giving her goose bumps. She rubbed her bare arms vigorously, certain it was the eerie morning that gave her the heebie-jeebies. But after several minutes of searching through the forest without finding Reena, Lizzie's fears rose to panic level. Her throat hurt from calling the dog and everything looked the same, leaving her directionally challenged in the dark.

Should she return to the house and ask for Walker's help before she got lost? She scanned the shadowed woodland where the trees stood close together, and the leaves overhead blocked out the beginning rays of early-morning sunlight.

No, she couldn't leave her partner behind. Yet if there was danger ahead, Lizzie was unarmed. If she encountered a wild animal, she'd have no recourse or defense. Bears and mountain lions weren't often seen roaming the grounds, but that didn't mean it never happened.

Terror constricted her throat, and her worst imaginings clouded her judgment. She shook off the images. "Reena!" Lizzie whistled and the sound echoed around her.

She paused and surveyed the path she'd taken. Perhaps returning home for her gun was wise. She chastised herself for forgetting it before leaving the house. Lizzie never went anywhere without her duty weapon. The lack of sleep had compromised her preparedness.

A whimper carried on the wind, and Lizzie spun on her heel in search of the source. "Reena?" Was her sweet dog injured? "Reena!"

Instantly, Lizzie hurried deeper into the forest, eyes flicking wildly in all directions, desperate to find her dog.

Lizzie rushed between two massive evergreens and stepped on something rough.

Suddenly the ground whipped from beneath her, sending Lizzie airborne. She screamed, flailing her arms in search of purchase.

She landed with a thud, whooshing the air from her lungs on the hard earth. Lizzie stared at the canopy of tree branches above, gasping to catch her breath.

The sound of footsteps approached.

She looked to the left just as someone wrapped her in dark

fabric, engulfing her in a papoose-style hold. He'd moved so fast, Lizzie hadn't a chance to react. He'd bound her arms tight against her side, and she could scarcely breathe. Worse, the material covered her face, prohibiting her from seeing.

Then she was in the air again as strong hands hoisted her upright. Lizzie screamed, wriggling and kicking with all her might to try and free herself. The confining fabric was unrelenting, and her efforts drained her energy. The kidnapper tossed her onto his shoulder, inverting Lizzie. The impact hurt her wounded rib from the last attack, and she cried out in pain.

He said nothing.

Not a word.

He clutched her legs tightly, and Lizzie gasped against the pressure on her injured ribs. She sucked in an excruciating inhale, then grunted, "Why are you doing this? What do you want? Who are you? Where is my dog?" The questions tumbled out rapid-fire.

He offered no response, but his respiration came out in hard pants as though carrying her was a struggle. Lizzie tried again, doing her best to flail her body and ignore the pain in her chest. She twisted, determined to make her abduction as difficult if not impossible for her kidnapper.

It worked! The man dropped her, and she landed face-first. Thankfully the material provided a thin cushion between her chin and the ground.

Lizzie stretched her arm away from her side, loosening the confining fabric. The possibility of freeing herself motivated Lizzie and she fought harder.

Something pinched her between her shoulder blades.

She yelped, but the sound seemed to evaporate. The minimal section of material that had shifted provided her a slit of vision. The image of the rocky ground blurred.

Lizzie blinked rapidly, desperate to clear her sight. "Whady—" Her question melted into a single slurred word before falling away from her lips.

Realization slammed into her.

He'd drugged her. Why wait until he'd gotten her wrapped up? Was he hiding his identity or improvising on his plan?

Lizzie tried to wriggle free, but her limbs refused to cooperate. She couldn't move her body.

Footsteps approached, and a large brown boot stood in front of her face.

Still her abductor said not a word.

And the ground spun.

Then everything went dark.

SEVEN

Walker awakened on the sofa and crept down the hall, spotting the spare room and Lizzie's closed bedroom door. The sun had started to rise, so it was still early. He'd let Kelan and Lizzie sleep and work on breakfast after he freshened up. He headed to the garage apartment to get ready for the day and returned to the kitchen to start breakfast, then hesitated. They'd all worked long hours. A little extra sleep wouldn't kill them.

Walker scrolled through his emails and caught up on admin work.

After making a pot of coffee, his phone buzzed with a text from Captain Cole. He'd included Vandeaux on the message.

Otho Mace was killed in a prison fight eight months ago with rival biker gang members.

Vandeaux's response beat Walker's reply. Thanks.

That eliminated Mace from the suspect list.

Walker checked his watch. Time to wake Kelan and Lizzie. He walked down the hall and rapped on her door first. "Wake up sleepyhead." He listened for a response but heard nothing. Worry had him knocking harder on the door. "Lizzie? Reena?"

Silence.

He repeated the actions on the spare room, again hearing nothing. He gripped the knob and peeked into Lizzie's room and the spare room. Both were empty. Where had they gone? And why hadn't they awakened him?

Walker texted both repeatedly, waiting eagerly for a response. Where'd you two go?

Kelan finally replied forty minutes later. Court today. Meeting with DA. Be back at the manhunt as soon as I'm finished.

Wait, what? Lizzie was alone? He checked the text, confirming her message remained on delivered status.

Again, Walker messaged Kelan. Where's Lizzie?

No response. *Okay, deep breath.* Worry sent Walker storming out the front door, where he immediately noticed the missing police cruiser. Was the officer reassigned? Lizzie had mentioned they were short on personnel with the manhunt. Her vehicle sat in the driveway and Kelan's was gone.

Why hadn't he realized Kelan left? Probably because he'd overslept. Mentally smacking himself, Walker rushed inside and slid on his shoulder holster and duty weapon. He sent another text to Kelan. Was the cruiser here when you left?

No bubbles appeared on the screen. Why wasn't Kelan answering?

Walker ran his hands over his head then exited the house. He glanced at the front door. He didn't have a key, and he didn't feel comfortable leaving it unlocked. But he'd have to for now.

He aimed for the foothills at the far side of the property. If she'd taken Reena out, she might've forgotten her phone in the house. He should've checked before he left, but going back would consume precious time if she was in trouble.

Reena was with her. That was a little comforting. Regardless, Walker's instincts warned something wasn't right.

He quickened his pace and called out, "Lizzie?"

No response.

Walker's pulse raced with fear and all the possible unknowns. After calling for Lizzie and Reena several more times without any reply, his panic ratcheted into full force. He approached a dense section of trees. Using his phone's flashlight app since the foliage blocked much of the sunlight working to permeate through the evergreens, he proceeded deeper into the forest.

He'd walked about five hundred yards when he spotted the unmoving pile of fur.

Walker sprinted to where Reena lay, her tongue lolling to one side and eyes closed. "Please don't be dead." He touched her torso, and the steady rise and fall of her breaths brought relief. He surveyed the area. Lizzie wouldn't leave Reena unattended; likewise, the dog's loyalty kept her glued to Lizzie's side.

Walker gently examined the canine for injuries. He rolled her over, locating the small tranquilizer dart still stuck in her hind leg near her tail. Walker removed the offensive weapon. "Lizzie?" Even as he called her name, Walker knew she'd not reply.

He lifted Reena just as gunshots exploded around him. Walker flattened on the ground, covering her, and took cover behind a huge stone between two evergreens. He withdrew his firearm, waiting for the shooter.

Silence.

Then a bullet pelted the dirt on the other side of the boulder.

Walker crouched low, squatting behind the protective barrier, and returned fire.

After several rounds, the gunshots ceased.

Walker took the opportunity to hoist the unconscious retriever into his arms. He rushed to the house, taking a route most concealed by the forest.

When he reached the edge of the clearing, he paused. He'd have no protection in the space between the woodland and Lizzie's house. But he had no choice. Reena was injured and he needed backup. He stepped out into the glade, walking a hundred yards before the gunfire resumed.

The shooter was following him.

Walker darted to the side, zigzagging between trees and boulders, then moving closer to the road, until he finally reached the house and ducked inside for safety.

He gently placed Reena on the sofa and called Captain Cole. When Cole answered, Walker blurted, "Lizzie's missing and

Reena was tranquilized. Active shooter in the foothills. Request backup."

"On the way," Cole replied.

Next, Walker contacted Kelan, who didn't answer and hadn't responded to Walker's text messages. No doubt he'd had to silence his phone while meeting with the DA, since it was too early for court to have started.

Walker replayed the earlier text from Kelan. He'd claimed to have a meeting with the DA. Kelan was with Walker and Lizzie most of the time at the house, but he'd on more than one occasion returned late from manhunt responsibilities. He'd had access to Lizzie. He could've tranquilized Reena and put her in the closet, then tried to abduct Lizzie. Was it possible Walker's old friend was a dirty cop?

What if he'd lied about attending court this morning to kidnap Lizzie? Except why was Reena deep in the forest?

Another intrusive thought entered his mind.

Was Kelan avoiding Walker? Why would he do that? Only one reason.

Kelan was involved in the kidnapping attempts.

No, that was ludicrous. He trusted his friend, and they'd worked together for years. Kelan would never get mixed up with convicts. However, they'd agreed the mastermind behind the prisoners' escapes might be someone the convicts feared. Kelan worked in a position of power.

Images of Zeke bounced to Walker's mind. He thought he'd known Zeke, too, and never imagined he'd be involved in a shooting gone wrong then ask Lizzie to cover up his crime.

Walker called Vandeaux, who answered immediately. "Where's Kelan?"

"Hello to you, too," his boss replied sarcastically. "He's got court and a meeting with the DA."

"Yeah, yeah, he told me that, too, but do you *know* where he is?"

"Walker, slow down, what're you saying?"

"He's gone and won't answer my texts. Lizzie is missing and Reena was tranquilized again." Walker provided a brief recap, pacing frantically.

"Before you make a hasty accusation, think about what you're implying." The warning that hovered in Vandeaux's voice gave Walker pause.

Was he being irrational?

"Start at the beginning," Vandeaux urged.

Walker explained his reasoning.

"I can see where you'd put those pieces together, however, I trust Kelan and cannot fathom that he'd do something so nefarious and risk his existence, his career or Lizzie's life. So, I'm going to insist you exhaust all possibilities before making such life-altering accusations."

Walker worked his jaw, irritated.

"In the meantime," Vandeaux continued, "I'll verify with the DA that he met with Kelan and get back to you."

"Understood," Walker ground out between clenched teeth.

At the moment he didn't care about his career or anyone but Lizzie. Worry for her was all that motivated him.

Reena fidgeted beside him, gaining Walker's attention. She yawned and stretched lethargically on the sofa. "Hey, girl." Walker knelt next to her as she slowly came to. "Take it easy," he soothed, unsure what to do.

Hurry up, Cole. He mentally urged the captain to get there faster.

Reena slid off the couch, swaying slightly. She stumbled a few steps, still groggy, and headed for her water bowl. Reena needed a vet. Maybe Cole would have a suggestion. Someone who could come to the house. After lapping, she faced him. He was no veterinarian, but she looked okay.

The roar of an engine approached, and Walker rushed to the front door. He sighed relief at Cole's unit pulling into the driveway. Walker glanced at his watch. Only ten minutes had passed since he'd made the call, yet it had seemed to take forever.

The captain and an officer Walker recognized as the one stationed outside the house earlier exited the vehicle, along with a man dressed in jeans and a T-shirt, carrying a medical bag. Walker whipped open the door and closed the distance to them. "Where were you?" he bellowed.

The young police officer, most likely still a rookie, blinked. "What? Deputy US Marshal Kelan Evans called me because he had a flat tire. I assisted him."

Cole shook his head. "You should've notified Walker before you left."

The officer glanced down, his face flushed red.

"You saw Kelan? He was alone?"

"Yes. I helped him change his tire and he drove away."

"What time did that happen?" Walker demanded.

"A couple of hours ago."

Walker processed the timeline in his mind. The problem was he didn't know when Lizzie had gone missing. Kelan's tire incident might've hindered backup getting to Lizzie. Was it a setup to give him an alibi?

"This is Matt, our family vet," Cole said. "Thought he could examine Reena."

Matt gave a nod. "Is she inside?"

Walker nodded. "In the living room."

Matt moved past them and entered the house.

"Whoever abducted Lizzie hasn't kept her for very long." Walker led them back inside while updating them on the morning's events. "I believe the shooter is still in the vicinity."

"Unless he hid a vehicle," Cole said. He gestured to the golden. "If anyone can find her, it's Reena."

"She's still woozy," Walker said, unsure why he was arguing.

Matt nodded from the living room. "She's fine. The tranquilizer must've been a light dose if she's up and moving already. They've pretty much worn off."

"Good, because she's the only hope we have," Walker said. "I've watched Lizzie work with her while we trekked through the mountains on the manhunt. I don't know if she'll listen to me, but it's worth a try."

"Grab a scent article," Cole suggested.

"Right." Why hadn't he thought of that? Walker had to get his mind back to marshal mode and out of worry-for-Lizzie mode. He hurried to her room, opting for a pillowcase, removed it, then returned to the living room and presented it to the dog. "Reena, find." He used the command as he remembered Lizzie doing.

She smelled the fabric, tail wagging, and he reiterated the order. "Find Lizzie."

Reena moved the door, indicating she was ready to work. He snapped on her lead and again offered the scent article, then proceeded outside.

To his amazement, Reena took off like a racehorse, forcing Walker to run behind her with the leash fully extended. She headed for the woods, and he glanced over his shoulder to where Cole and the rookie cop trailed him at a distance. Certain Reena was returning to where he'd found her, he was surprised when she tugged the lead away from the area.

Walker kept up with her, giving her the length necessary to work.

When she approached a wider path where tire tracks were embedded deep in the dusty earth, Reena stopped and sat. Walker caught up to her and surveyed the landscape and the tracks. Smaller tires, most likely a utility vehicle, which would easily maneuver over the rugged terrain.

Cole and the rookie jogged to his side, Cole panting. "Why did you stop?"

Walker pointed to the ground. "Someone parked a four-wheeler here."

Cole paced, circling the space. "Reena can't track any farther because the kidnapper drove off with Lizzie!"

Walker lifted his phone. No call or text from Vandeaux. He called Kelan's number again and started for Lizzie's house. Cole barked orders into his shoulder mic and at the rookie behind him.

Kelan answered on the second ring, but Walker didn't give him a chance to speak. "Where's Lizzie?"

"What're you talking about?"

"Where are you? Why didn't you answer?"

"I left for court early this morning. Lizzie was outside with Reena. She promised to go into the house when Reena had finished."

"You saw and talked to Lizzie before you left?"

"Yes. She was fine. Why? What's going on?"

"What else happened this morning?" Walker pressed.

"I got a flat tire on the interstate driving to the DA's office. Barely made my meeting with him and we just finished."

Walker paused, his heart thrumming hard. It would be easy to blame his friend, but Vandeaux's warning hung in the back of his mind.

"Walker. Breathe, man. Calm down. What's going on?"

"What time did you see Lizzie before you left?"

"About five o'clock. The cruiser was out front, and Lizzie was waiting on Reena."

"Why didn't you stay with her?"

"She insisted she was fine and Reena wouldn't be long. Besides, you were still at the house." Kelan's tone grew harder. "What're you implying?"

"You were the last to see her. What happened? Did she figure out you were working with the escapees? Threatened to turn you in like she did Zeke Doland? You had to shut her up. Convenient it all transpired while I was asleep, right? Then you just happen to be busy and don't answer your phone in the time we're searching for her. Where are you now?" The accusations tumbled out of Walker's face faster than he processed them.

"Walker, I get that you're upset, but you'd better think hard about your next words. I've been out of pocket because I had a flat tire. The Bison Valley PD officer came to help me, which is why he wasn't in front of the house. Ask him. I don't know why he didn't tell you that before he left. I couldn't respond to your texts because I was in with the DA. Vandeaux called before you did, and I was about to return your call. I need to go into court now, but I'll head that way as soon as I'm done."

Walker didn't reply.

"Look, I understand you're stressed because you care about Lizzie. I'll remind you that I'm your friend and I value my job. There's GPS tracking on my unit, and there are security cameras at the DA's office and the courthouse, verifying my presence in both places. I'll ignore the nonsense you spewed at me."

Everything Kelan said was provable. He ran his hand over his head. "I'm sorry. I'm outta my mind with worry."

"You're crazy about her, aren't you?"

Walker gaped at the phone.

"I get it. She's into you, too."

"I—"

"Lizzie was well when I left her, but I'll head back and help with the search. Breathe, man. And before you go all guns and accusations blazing, pray. You need wisdom, not raw emotion guiding you."

"You're right. I'm sorry."

They disconnected and Walker paced the house. He should've awakened before Lizzie. It was his job to stay with her. Why had she gone outside without him? Because he was lazy and overslept. A niggle of memory reminded Walker that Kelan had mentioned the meeting with the district attorney and court today. In the chaos, Walker had forgotten those details. He ran his hand over his head again. How had he failed Lizzie this bad? He never should've agreed to let her stay on the case after the first attack. Of course, the kidnapper had waited for the perfect opportunity. Walker had delivered Lizzie on a platter of ignorance by not guarding her. Why hadn't he insisted on protective custody? What would he do if anything happened to her?

Walker's stomach roiled and helplessness consumed him with such force it nearly dropped him to his knees. He plopped onto the chair on the porch and plunged his head into his hands. "Please, God, help me find her. Protect her, please." Because when he found Lizzie, he would tell her that nothing had changed. He was still in love with her, and he'd never again let her go. He prayed he'd get a second chance.

Fear coursed through Walker at levels he'd never experienced before. Where was Lizzie? Someone had been relentless in trying to kidnap her. He never should've left her alone. Not for an instant. He'd neglected her and failed to do his job. And after all these years, he should've been braver and told her that he cared about her. He'd never stopped. What if he never got the chance? What if—

He looked at Reena again. He had to find Lizzie. He snapped Reena's leash and harness on once more. "Come on, girl. We must find Lizzie. And fast."

Lizzie groaned, dragging herself from the depths of darkness. The hard floor spun beneath her as though she sat on a merry-go-round, taking her back to her childhood. She squinted against the brightness that broke through a sliver of space between her nose and the red fabric covering her eyes. Lizzie squeezed them shut again, straining from the sensation that the world was whirling her into a blur. She shifted to grasp something only to discover her wrists were bound behind her.

Terror had Lizzie's eyes flicking open. She screamed, but her desperation died in the fabric stuffed in her mouth. Her breaths came out in short, quick bursts, rising panic within her.

Trying to gain her bearings, she chided herself with self-soothing advice to breathe slower before she hyperventilated. She peered through the small opening at the bottom of her blindfold and blinked to clear her vision. Her gaze traveled to her ankles, secured with gray duct tape just above her bare feet. Apparently, she'd lost her flip-flops somewhere. She wiggled her fingers and decided the same adhesive bound her wrists. The restraints forced her to move like a caterpillar. Lizzie worm-crawled to a sitting position and, using her shoulder and right knee, pushed the blindfold higher and glimpsed her prison.

She tilted her head, studying the log walls, and surmised she was in a deserted cabin. Dirt and old wood scents tickled her nose, and she sneezed. On the plus side, her captor wasn't present, but was he watching through a hidden camera lens? Lizzie listened to the muted birdsongs filtering into the stuffy space. She inched closer to the wall and noticed the window above her head. Images of Reena whimpering returned, and her heart drummed hard against her ribs. Was her sweet dog okay? Had he hurt Reena? She had to get out of here.

Worry for her partner and fear for what the abductor intended to do to her motivated Lizzie to escape. She scoured her memory for cabins near her property, mentally traversing the grounds. Nothing. *Think, Lizzie.* If the kidnapper had taken her on foot, he couldn't have gone far from her house. But why do that? It would be too easy to locate him.

From the recesses of her foggy mind, the sound of a small engine, like a four-wheeler, returned. Yes! He'd placed on her something and sped away. What cabin was within a UTV's distance from her property?

Once on a hike with Reena, she'd spotted a river that tore through the foothills north of her place, and she recalled a faded image of a dilapidated structure, more shed than cabin. That must be her current location.

The sour aroma of ammonia and rot wafted to her from a

rancid armchair beside her. Scratching from what she assumed were mice living inside the cushions encouraged Lizzie to scoot away on the wood floor.

She shivered and turned, searching for a tool to free herself. The chair was the only furniture in the single room. Lizzie repositioned herself to gain a different view of the space and noticed the window was broken. Had whoever left her here presumed she'd not awaken before he returned? Where had he gone?

An involuntary shudder sent Lizzie's imagination in terrifying directions. Her contemplations were halted by a voice outside, in the distance. If only she could get to her feet, she'd look outside. She couldn't fight with her hands behind her back, and running with her ankles bound wasn't an option.

Think.

Someone was talking, but to who? Lizzie strained to hear.

A woman's voice, and based on the increasing volume, she was moving closer.

Lizzie leaned closer to the window, desperate to glean information. She couldn't decipher the words, but the speaker's tone conveyed agitation.

Who was she? There were only males listed on the prison escapees list. However, a female associate wasn't inconceivable.

"No!" the woman hollered.

Perhaps an unwilling accomplice. Once Lizzie reminded her that holding an officer of the law was a federal crime with heavy repercussions, she'd release Lizzie.

"I never agreed to kill a cop!"

The words froze the blood in Lizzie's veins.

Staccato footsteps paced on what Lizzie assumed was a wooden porch outside the window.

"No." A pause. "Forget it. I'm not doing that."

Silence.

The steps stopped and the knob turned.

Sunlight beamed through the open door, which nearly smacked

into Lizzie. She collapsed to the ground quickly, sitting against the wall with her knees pulled up and ducking her head, hiding her face.

She sucked in a breath.

The door closed and the woman walked across the cabin. Lizzie debated whether to look at her kidnapper, but without more information, she didn't move.

The woman approached Lizzie, and she spotted running shoes through the shifted blindfold.

"I never agreed to this," she said. "I know you're listening. Please turn around and I'll remove the gag."

Lizzie did as instructed. The woman pulled the blindfold down, securing it over Lizzie's eyes, then removed the gag and tape in one swift tug. Lizzie's mouth stung, but she gasped, inhaling oxygen and filling her lungs. "Thank you," she rasped. "Please, help me. You said yourself you don't want to hurt me."

No reply. Was she considering Lizzie's plea?

"Look, I haven't seen your face, so I can't identify you. I'm a law enforcement officer. Think about your future." An engine rumbled, and Lizzie's pulse quickened. "Release me. I'll tell the authorities you rescued me."

Her captor refused to respond, and when a car door slammed beyond the log walls, Lizzie grew desperate.

"I can only buy you time. For now, pretend you're unconscious or he'll kill you," the woman hissed.

Lizzie rolled to her side as quick footfalls thudded on the other side of the door. It whipped open and a man hollered, "Let's go!"

"What about her? She's still out cold," the woman lied.

Lizzie fought to breathe slow and steady. He crossed the room to her, and she nearly flinched when fingers pressed against her neck.

"I didn't say she was dead." Her tone was sarcastic, but it worked, and he withdrew his touch. "You gave her too much of the drug."

"I did not. I'll be back to deal with her." Something in his voice sounded familiar. Where had Lizzie heard it before?

"Whatever. Just leave me out of it."

A pause, then they exited the cabin.

Two car doors slammed, and the engine roared to life, then sped away.

Though Lizzie wanted to jump to her feet, she couldn't, and she wasn't sure it was safe. She waited, counted to a hundred, and considered the woman had never mentioned to her partner that she'd removed Lizzie's gag. She'd been facing the wall, but he'd touched her neck. Had he noticed?

She must escape before he returned to finish her off. Lizzie pushed herself to a sitting position again. With all her strength, she pressed her back against the log walls and inched to her feet. Something sharp grazed her finger, and she flinched at the pain, jolting away.

She used the tip of her finger to search for the offensive object. Several nails protruded from the wood. Perfect. Lizzie positioned her wrists over the nail heads and jerked them downward, tearing the adhesive and her skin simultaneously. Encouraged by the success, she ignored the stinging and repeated the action four times, freeing her hands.

Lizzie tore off the blindfold, getting a full view of the dilapidated cabin while ripping the tape around her ankles. Without hesitation, she grabbed the doorknob and burst into the fresh air.

In two steps, she bounded off the porch, stumbling and catching herself before she fell onto the pinecone–covered path. Rocks pierced her bare feet, but she didn't have time to whine about that. The overgrown lane had fresh tire marks that led away from the cabin. If she walked out to the road, she might intersect with the kidnapper. Lizzie turned and surveyed the wilderness surrounding the structure.

Better to take her chances in the thick forest. Without a compass, Lizzie was uncertain where she was or which way to go. And if she got lost out there…

She didn't allow herself to finish the intrusive thought.

Distance was her only defense.

Lizzie sprinted into the woods, stepping over the tall scrub brush and trekking the rocky ground. Whatever drug they'd injected her with still coursed through her system, and the effects caused her to stumble off balance more than a few times. But she didn't stop.

Caught between terror and resolve, Lizzie hurried forward.

She climbed the rising terrain, her breaths labored as she sought purchase for her feet in the dry earth.

Behind her the sounds of an engine carried on the wind.

No. He'd returned already.

Fear stabbed Lizzie's heart. She glanced at the foothill in front of her. Whatever was on the other side would either help her or be her death.

She scaled faster, gripping the weeds, rocks and tree branches, pulling herself higher. The steep incline made it challenging to move quickly. Her feet skidded on the pebbly ground, and she slipped, slamming hard against the stones protruding from the mountainside. Lizzie regained her hold and grasped at a young tree trunk, then climbed past it.

A man's holler reached her.

"You can't run," he called.

Footsteps rushed toward her, but Lizzie didn't look back. She crested the foothill and spotted movement below. Quickly she ducked and turned to make her descent.

Evergreens and aspens tightly knit together provided places for Lizzie to zigzag through. She stayed on the pine needle–covered surface to prevent making indentations in the soil.

Then, as often as possible, she hid behind boulders and thick brambles, watching for her pursuer.

His threats stopped.

It was all too quiet.

Unsure whether he'd given up or was still in pursuit, Lizzie kept moving. Distance was her only hope of survival.

Then, in her peripheral, she saw his silhouetted form cresting the foothill.

Lizzie scurried deeper into the woods and gave up trying to hide her path.

Footsteps, whether hers or his she couldn't tell, closed in on her.

The sound echoed.

Weak and still battling the effects of the drugs in her system, Lizzie ducked, hiding behind a boulder. Maybe outrunning him wasn't feasible. If he had personal knowledge of the area, he'd outsmart her.

She'd retaliate. But with what? Surely, he was armed.

Lizzie glanced to the side. Was she going the correct way?

Tears pricked her eyes, and she shoved them down. No, she couldn't fall apart right now.

Suddenly what sounded like a rush of footsteps filled the atmosphere.

More than one? Were they surrounding her? What if the man's accomplice had set her up? Was this a twisted game?

She didn't have much time.

Lizzie scanned the ground closest to her in search of a weapon.

A large stone half buried near the tree offered promise. With her fingernails, Lizzie dug the object free, then squatted behind the boulder and waited.

Lizzie held her breath. Unmoving.

The steps hurried toward her.

When they'd drawn as close as Lizzie dared, she inhaled, lifting the stone.

She had one weapon. A single chance to fight back.

If she missed... No, that wasn't an option.

The steps hesitated.

Lizzie crouched lower and willed him to approach.

Panting nearby gave her the cue.

With a prayer for courage, Lizzie hoisted the rock overheard.

She leaped to her feet and, bellowing a primal war cry, Lizzie heaved the stone at her pursuer.

EIGHT

Reena barked and jerked to the side with a yelp, forcing Walker away from the boulder. Her quick reaction helped him narrowly dodge the flying rock and blonde blur that launched at him. Both landed with a thud next to his boots and the place where he'd stood only moments before. He reached for his gun, dropping the leash, and prepared to fire.

He blinked, focusing on his attacker. "Lizzie?"

She stumbled forward, obviously dazed and confused. Her cheeks and forehead were smeared with dark smudges. Her clothes, once a white T-shirt and light blue joggers, were now covered in dirt. Grime streaked the fabric, and scrapes marred her bare feet.

Reena barreled for her partner, tail wagging and barking happily in greeting. Lizzie dropped to her knees and planted her face in the flurry of fur. "You found me."

"Lizzie, are you okay?" Walker stepped forward and holstered his weapon.

She didn't lift her head.

"Please, tell me you're all right." He knelt beside her. "What happened?" Walker moved closer but didn't interrupt the happy reunion.

Finally, Lizzie glanced up, tears marbling her cheeks in dark rivers. "I escaped."

Walker pulled her into his arms, and she melted in wracking sobs. "You're safe. I've got you." Even as he said the words, he felt like a liar. If he'd done his job, this never would've happened. It was his fault. He'd failed her, and he didn't want to imagine what she'd been through. He didn't press her to talk, rather, he held her as she cried. Whether from relief or fear he wasn't sure.

She withdrew and sat back on her heels. The angst in her green eyes tore through to his heart.

"I was daydreaming while Reena roamed the yard, and before I knew it, she'd disappeared. I couldn't find her, then I stepped onto this fabric, and he wrapped it around me." Her words tumbled out fast in one incomplete sentence.

"Who?"

"The man—" she hiccupped "—grabbed me. He drugged me and when I woke up, I was in a cabin." She whipped around as though suddenly searching for someone. "He followed me." She jumped to her feet. "We have to go."

Walker didn't argue. They started back to her house. He'd not seen a pursuer following her or even encountered another human while trekking through the forest. Now he constantly scanned for danger. Lizzie held Reena's leash, keeping her close, which allowed him to keep his gun at the ready.

"You're barefoot," Walker reminded Lizzie.

She glanced down and shrugged. "Doesn't matter."

They made it to the creek, and the icy current reached their knees. Reena tromped through it, undeterred, while Walker gingerly assisted Lizzie to the other side. The last thing she needed was to get hypothermia.

"How'd you find me?" She glanced at the water, reiterating the dog should've lost her scent.

"I saw the indentation farther down from the four-wheeler and knew he'd driven across the stream," Walker explained.

"Reena, you're so smart," Lizzie said, but she didn't stop walking. The dog wagged her tail in approval. "There was a woman working with him."

Walker put a hand on her shoulder. "What?"

"Don't stop." She shrugged off his touch and question.

The gesture stung, but he kept pace with her. When they'd created distance from the boulder where Lizzie had attacked him, she said, “She didn’t cut off the restraints—”

“You were bound?” Walker clarified.

“Yes, duct tape, the choice of all criminals,” she quipped, and despite the seriousness of the situation, he smiled. “I got free and ran. But he chased me.”

Walker again surveyed the surroundings. “Maybe he saw us and turned around.” Yet he couldn’t shake the feeling someone watched them. “You mentioned a woman?”

“Yes, she made me turn my back to her. I was blindfolded. She said she didn’t sign up to kill a cop.”

Fury roiled through Walker, and he fought to maintain his calm. “What else?”

“That was it. When he showed up—”

“Did you see him?” Hope that they’d finally identify the kidnapper encouraged Walker’s pace.

“No, but his voice, it was familiar.” Her eyebrows knit together in contemplation.

“As in you know him?”

“Yes. No. I don’t know. It was—”

“Familiar,” Walker concluded.

“Yes.”

They hiked deeper into the thickening forest, forcing Walker to push aside the low-hanging branches to create a path. They passed through the evergreens and progressed toward the trail he recognized. “What else?”

“She told me to pretend I was still unconscious, then he showed up and they left. But I never saw either of them.”

“Did you recognize her voice?”

Lizzie considered the question. “I… I don’t know.” She paused and faced him, brows peaked.

“We’ll figure this out together.” Unable to restrain himself, Walker pulled her into his arms. “Thank God you’re okay.”

“I will be.” She withdrew. “I want to go home.”

"Lizzie, we can't. Your place isn't safe."

"But don't you see? That means they'll keep coming. Their stupidity makes them easier to catch. We'll get them."

"No, we need to move to a safe house."

"No." Lizzie vehemently shook her head. "We have to catch them, and we can't do that from a safe house."

Walker groaned. Her reasoning reminded Walker they were coworkers. Nothing else. He must rein in his emotions. But losing Lizzie and subsequently finding her was overwhelming; his mind and heart hadn't fully processed the events.

Reena led the way and Walker spotted relief on Lizzie's face once she saw her home through the clearing. The Bison Valley PD cruiser had resumed patrolling and sat parked in the driveway. He'd begged Captain Cole to let him work alone with Reena in case Lizzie returned on her own. Reluctantly, the man had agreed.

They entered the house, and Reena flopped onto her dog bed. Walker messaged Captain Cole and Emmett as soon as he got service. Found Lizzie. She's okay.

Emmett called first and Walker provided a synopsis. "I don't have details. Lizzie's in the bathroom, cleaning up." Just as he spoke the words, the shower turned on. He stayed near her room, unwilling to give the kidnapper any opportunity for a repeat performance.

"I'll update Cole. Vandeaux has offered a safe house for the two of you," Emmett added.

Walker had expected nothing less. "Thank you." They disconnected and he heard the water shut off. He slumped onto the sofa and stroked Reena's fur. Without her help, he couldn't imagine what would've happened to Lizzie. Regardless, staying here wasn't an option.

Lizzie entered wearing clean clothes with her hair wrapped in a towel.

"I was a mess," she said.

"You should have a doctor examine you."

"Why? I have a few cuts and bruises, but nothing significant." She pinned him with a stubborn look.

He relented, concluding he had a bigger fight to wage with her. "Cole told me Mace was killed in prison eight months ago."

Lizzie blew out a long breath. "That eliminates him from the suspect list."

"Yes."

"We're back to the last three convicts, then."

Walker used the comment to launch his plan. "I've arranged for us to move to a safe house. We cannot stay here. There are too many unknowns."

She paused, and he anticipated her fury. Instead, she said, "You're right. Okay."

Relieved he wouldn't have to justify the relocation order, yet saddened by her resignation, Walker asked, "Do you remember anything about your abductors?"

"Nothing more than what I've shared. She seemed reluctant to work with him and even scolded him for giving me too much of the drug."

"She must have medical knowledge about the correct dosage."

"Right." Lizzie exhaled. "I wonder if he didn't have her voluntary compliance."

"Coerced?"

"Possibly? Blackmailed? Fear? There's a lot of reasons," Lizzie said. "Or maybe he wanted to take the abduction further than she did."

"As in kill you?"

"Yes."

Walker swallowed hard as a fresh wave of guilt assuaged him again. "It never should've happened. If I'd been with you, they wouldn't have had the opportunity to get to you."

"Walker, I took Reena out for a potty break. Kelan offered to wake you since he had to leave, and I refused. I should've called

Reena back and done my daydreaming in the house. I'm the one who made the wrong choice," Lizzie argued.

"No, if I'd been awake and stayed with you—"

"You're blaming yourself for resting?" Lizzie shook her head. "I accept responsibility for my actions. I thought I was safe on my property with the officer keeping watch. I should've known better. I assumed it was too early in the morning for an attacker." She laughed sardonically.

"Lizzie—"

She held up her hand. "It's not your fault."

"I failed you." Walker looked down, wanting to confess his feelings. Recalling the way she'd twice shied away from his touch, he shoved down the untimely emotions and focused on the case. "Regardless, let's combine our data." Walker moved the whiteboard and Lizzie joined him. "I'll pull Juhl, Arnold and Herrera's information to see if they recently married or had women visitors."

"I can do that on the drive to the safe house."

They gathered supplies for Lizzie and Reena. Walker threw his go-bag together and received a text from Vandeaux with the address.

Within ten minutes, they'd loaded into his vehicle.

Once they were on the road, she asked, "Where are we going?"

"Manitou Springs." He held out his cell phone, showing her the map. "Keeps us close enough to stay involved in the manhunt and far enough from your house so the kidnappers can't trace our location."

"Works for me." Lizzie pulled her laptop from the case and typed while he drove.

"Both Juhl and Arnold are married."

"How about stopping for lunch while we make those inquiries? I'd prefer not to do that from our destination."

"Think they'll trace the calls?"

"Dunno, but we won't give them opportunity." He pulled into

a Mexican restaurant, where delicious smells had Lizzie's stomach growling.

"There's patio seating," she said, leashing Reena.

They entered the restaurant and Lizzie requested to sit outside. The hostess showed them to a table in the corner. The place was nearly empty, giving them plenty of privacy.

Once they were seated and Reena was munching on her dog food, Lizzie and Walker split the list. Lizzie called Gregory Juhl's wife while Walker contacted Arnold's spouse. There was no answer on the number listed for her, so Walker dug deeper, locating a number for Arnold's mother. "This is Deputy US Marshal McCane," Walker began. "I was hoping to speak to Mr. Arnold's wife."

"She's not here and I haven't seen her in weeks. Don't call me again," the elderly woman snapped before hanging up.

"Well, that was a bust," he relayed to Lizzie.

"I got passed around to every member of the Juhl family, but none of them have heard from or seen his wife, either."

"As if we believe that." Walker grunted.

They had no evidence to request an all-points bulletin on either of the women, but their unavailability was suspicious.

"Adds to the possibility they're working together."

"It's not inconceivable that they'd help their husbands," Lizzie replied.

The waitress arrived with their food, halting their discussion.

"I didn't realize how hungry I was," Lizzie said, biting into a taco.

Walker swallowed his first bite. "That's amazing. Or I'm starving."

Lizzie chuckled. "A little of both, I'm guessing."

They finished eating, neither speaking, and paid the bill.

"We should grab burner phones to take to the house and power down our cell phones. I'd like to believe they're untraceable but—"

"—never underestimate criminals," Lizzie concluded.

Walker grinned. "Exactly." He drove to a big box store in Colorado Springs and purchased the disposable phones while Lizzie and Reena remained in the vehicle.

The trip to the safe house was quiet. Between the food and the physical and emotional exhaustion, they were both spent. Walker noticed how comfortable he felt in Lizzie's presence. As if talking wasn't necessary. He thought about Kelan's words. Was he missing the signs of her attraction to him?

"Looks like this is it." Lizzie gestured toward the long gravel driveway.

Trees lined the path to where the ranch-style house sat nestled among tall oaks. There wasn't a garage to conceal his car, but the property was located at the edge of the city limits. Additionally, the home and his SUV weren't visible from the road thanks to the abundance of foliage around them. He parked near the front door, and they unloaded the vehicle. Lizzie discovered the lockbox hidden beneath a planter and entered the code.

They did a full sweep of the premises before settling. The home had four bedrooms and two bathrooms. Simple decorations and adequate accommodations. Most importantly, it was clean and, thus far, free from danger.

They ventured to the back deck, where a glider and several chairs provided a comfortable resting area. Lizzie settled onto the porch swing, Reena at her feet. The dog hadn't left her side since the latest abduction attempt. Walker dropped onto a chair near the duo and called his dad.

He answered on the first ring. "Am I free?"

Walker smiled sadly. "Sorry, not quite yet. Just checking on you."

"I'm fine." His dad sighed. "Your friend Kelan just left."

Grateful for Kelan's help, Walker made a mental note to thank him. "He's a great guy."

"Yeah." A pause. "I can't stay like this much longer. I need to return to my life."

"We're doing everything to find the escapees, but the danger isn't lessening. It's imperative that you remain in the safe house for now."

"Walker, I have a job and responsibilities."

"I promise I'll be in touch soon." They disconnected and Walker's frustration mounted. He was failing the most important people around him.

Lizzie glanced his way. "Didn't go well?"

"He's sick of being under house arrest."

"I get that. I must shift gears and focus on the COK9 case. My CI, Dex, hasn't responded to me." She shook her head and withdrew her phone.

"He's aware of the danger of reporting on this Trigger person."

"Agreed. Which reaffirms I need to talk to him."

Walker eavesdropped as Lizzie placed the call. After a few seconds she frowned and set her device on her lap. "He's not answering. I didn't leave another message. I can't explain it, but my gut says something isn't right."

He wanted to offer supportive advice, but his experience with confidential informants was they weren't the most reliable people. Would they ever get a break in either case? His father's comment was dead-on—this couldn't go on forever. But if they couldn't catch the escaped convicts, what was the alternative?

The day passed uneventfully, and for that, Lizzie was grateful. Hard to believe that twenty-four hours earlier, she'd been kidnapped and held hostage in an abandoned cabin. She'd seen the guilt written on Walker's face and he'd attempted to apologize a hundred different ways. She couldn't get it through the man's thick head of hair that he wasn't at fault. She'd let down her guard, which nearly cost her and Reena their lives. But relying on another human for the rest of her life wasn't feasible.

Lizzie glanced at the nightstand clock and powered up her burner cell phone, calling Dex's number again. He'd proven a reliable CI in the past, but his lack of response upset Lizzie. The line rang twice before he answered. "Hey, Dex, it's Lizzie."

"I'll call you back." He hung up without clarification.

Lizzie stared at the cell phone as though it explained his strange reaction.

Within ten minutes, Dex called back. "What's up?"

"I've left several messages for you."

"Yeah. I'm busy."

Lizzie didn't press. "I need information on a guy named Trigger."

A long pause, then Dex said, "That's not an easy request."

"Why not?"

Dex lowered his voice. "He's not the kind of person you chat casually about. Whaddya want to know?"

"I'm working a case, and I have it on good authority that he's involved in kidnapping and killing pregnant teens and stealing their babies."

Dex gave a low whistle. "That's some nasty dirt, Lizzie."

"A pregnant teenager's life is in danger, Dex. If you have any information on Trigger's whereabouts or hangouts, I need it like yesterday."

A long pause.

"Dex?"

"Naw, you don't get it. What you're asking me to do is putting my safety on the line."

Lizzie sat up on the bed and leaned against the headboard. "Dex, you've gotta give me something. Please."

"First, pony up a small fortune, and add in witness protection for me to disappear before I go digging my own grave."

Hope had Lizzie's heart drumming. "You've got information?"

"Did you hear what I said?"

"Crystal clear, but before I do all that work, I have to tell my boss you've got solid intel."

"You ensure the details come together. I'll make it worth your while. Have I ever led you wrong?"

Lizzie had to admit Dex was the most reliable informant she'd encountered. "Can't say you have. However, your lack of response to my latest calls isn't something I'll tolerate moving forward."

"I understand. It was…extenuating circumstances." He sighed. "Get in touch when you've got it pulled together." He stated the amount of money he wanted, then disconnected.

Walker rapped on her open door. "Hey, I heard you talking. Everything okay?"

"Yeah, but for a second there I thought I worked for Dex."

Walker gave a sideways grin. "Demanding?"

"You could say that, but if it's legit intel, I can't refuse."

Curiosity hung in his handsome expression. "What does he want?"

"A lot of money and WitSec protection."

"Convenient." Walker crossed the room and dropped to sit in the chair near the closet. "Is he fabricating lies to escape his current life?"

Lizzie considered that. "It's possible. Dex is usually solid, but this last stint of ignoring my calls—"

"Yeah, how'd he explain that?"

"'Extenuating circumstances.'"

Walker shook his head. "What's that mean?"

"No clue. Could be anything from being hauled into jail to his girlfriend kicking him out of the house. With Dex, I can't even guess."

"But you trust him?"

"As far as you'd rely on any CI."

"Right. Let's see what we can do." Walker pushed to his feet.

"Wait, this isn't your case."

"Yeah, but if I can help, I'd like to. I'll make some calls."

"Thanks, Walker." Lizzie updated Emmett.

"He's our only lead, so I guess we'd better cough up the demands—if the intel is solid," the team leader said. "I'll tackle it and get back to you. You're safe, though?"

"We're at a house in—"

"Don't tell me. I only want confirmation you're protected," Emmett interrupted.

"We are."

"Good. I'll be in touch."

They disconnected, and she walked to the living room, Reena beside her. Lizzie appreciated the dog's presence.

She sprawled out on the sofa, overhearing Walker on his phone in the dining room. Lizzie glanced at the whiteboard with the escapees' information, thankful they'd thought to bring it along. She replayed everything she recalled from her time in the abandoned cabin. The man's voice had been familiar, but she couldn't place him. Who was it? And why would they want her? Why would the woman tell her to play dead? Had she encouraged the man to leave Lizzie, giving her the opportunity to escape? Once he realized she'd run away, had he harmed her?

Both Juhl's and Arnold's wives had petty charges, proving they'd been involved in offenses with their spouses. However, kidnapping and attempted murder of a police officer was a significant leap.

Reena nudged her arm with a soft whine. "Need a break, girl?" Lizzie pushed off the sofa and walked to where Walker spoke on the phone. She gestured toward Reena, and he nodded, getting to his feet while he continued the call.

They exited and relaxed on the deck as Reena explored the backyard, staying close to the house. The area was beautiful with no neighbors. Hidden against the mountainside, the residence provided a picturesque setting and tranquility.

"Thanks, I appreciate it." Walker hung up and joined her on the porch swing. "Doing okay?"

"Yeah, simply admiring this place."

"I'm uncertain how safe houses are chosen, yet I must admit this one of the better ones I've seen. It's almost like a vacation home."

Lizzie chuckled. "Wouldn't that be a surprise if it was, and the homeowners had no idea they'd housed two cops while they searched for escaped prisoners?"

"Probably wouldn't be a great feature on their sales brochure." Walker laughed.

Lizzie smiled at him. Admiring the way Walker joked easily with her as though they'd always been friends. She and Zeke had never shared lightheartedness in their relationship. He was intense and competitive. His presence alone sucked the fun from any room.

Her phone rang, and she glanced at the display. "It's Emmett."

"Good, I have an update for both of you."

She quickly swiped the screen. "Hey, Emmett, that was fast. I have Walker with me. Is speakerphone acceptable?"

"Yes."

Lizzie placed the device on speakerphone. "Go ahead."

"Hey, Walker, thanks again for moving Lizzie to a safe house. She's a valuable resource."

Lizzie's cheeks warmed at Emmett's compliment.

"Yes, she is. Happy to help." Walker glanced her way and butterflies danced in her stomach.

What was wrong with her? She averted her eyes.

"I spoke to Dodger, and if the intel is credible, he's agreed to personally pay the informant's fee," Emmett said.

"My boss also advised he'd handle the transfer of the informant into WitSec," Walker replied.

"Sounds like we're ready to roll," Emmett said.

"Great. I'll be in touch as soon as I get ahold of my CI." She disconnected. "Okay, let's hope he hasn't changed his mind." Lizzie called Dex again.

"Give me a sec." Dex hung up.

Walker flicked a curious glance her way. "Does he always talk to you like that?"

"No, this is new. But he's smart about finding a private place to converse." The line rang and Lizzie answered on speakerphone, pressing a finger to her lips for Walker to remain quiet. "All good?"

"Yeah, what's up?" Dex asked.

"Hey, everything is arranged as you requested—if your information is legit."

"Where do you want to meet?"

Lizzie and Walker shared a glance. "I'm knee-deep in another investigation so I can't connect face-to-face."

"No way, I'm not telling you anything over the phone."

"Text me?"

"No. You're not listening," Dex argued. "What I have to share will get me killed. I'll do it in person and then you take me to the safe house."

"Dex, I can't. You know you can trust me. I'm good for it."

"I don't think so. Not this time."

"I've got you covered." Lizzie exhaled a long breath and tried again. "The safe house, witness protection, everything. But Dex, I can't leave my current location. I'm in danger."

"Wait. What? No way, if you're in trouble—"

"It's not related to the adoption ring case, Dex," Lizzie assured him.

"For real?" Concern hovered in his tone.

For all his faults, Dex had been kind to her.

"Yes."

Dex sighed. "Fine. This is what I can tell you." Lizzie and Walker leaned closer to the phone, both laser focused on every word. "Trigger is pure evil."

"You make him sound diabolical," Lizzie replied. "He's a dirtbag criminal."

"Not even close. He's the worst kind. A slick operator who comes across as a nice, extremely helpful sort of guy. If Trigger is targeting pregnant girls and offering help, he'll easily convince them he's trustworthy. At the very least, they won't be immediately wary of him. He'd have no trouble kidnapping them."

"Expand on that. Specifically, what's his MO?" Lizzie asked.

"He'd win their confidence, persuade them they need him, and, like a cobra, he'll attack with a strike they never saw coming."

"Okay." Shivers ran up Lizzie's arms. "Any idea what he looks like? Name?"

"That's it, he's a chameleon. Blends in, very average and nondescript. He'd appear harmless, even passive."

That was the same description a pregnant checkout clerk had given Lizzie and Eli the month prior during their interview.

"That's all I'm saying over the phone. You bring the money and provide the safe house, and I'll give you the guy's real name."

"Dex—" Lizzie pleaded.

"No way," Dex replied. "I need insurance."

"Fine." Based on what he'd told her so far, Lizzie had no doubt Dex could identify Trigger. "Give me a little while to arrange a meeting time and obtain the funds. I'll text you the details." What had she agreed to?

"Hurry." Dex disconnected.

"I don't know, Lizzie," Walker said as she dialed Emmett.

"What choice do I have? This is the closest we've gotten." And she hoped Emmett approved.

Emmett answered, "That was fast."

"Yeah, listen to this." Lizzie relayed the information.

"That's a huge risk," Emmett said.

"And it's a significant lead," Lizzie contended.

"Fine, but you're not going alone, right, Walker?" Emmett asked.

Lizzie rolled her eyes at the not-so-subtle request.

"Correct." Walker smiled. "I'll accompany her."

"And we'll have our team watching, too," Emmett added. "Just in case your kidnapper or CI tries playing us."

"My buddy Kelan is the DUSM who will escort the CI into WitSec if, and only if, the information he provides proves worthy," Walker advised.

Could Walker have used any more abbreviations if he'd tried?

"Sounds good," Emmett said. "I'll be in touch. Let me work out the details."

Once they'd disconnected, Lizzie addressed Walker, "Thank you for making arrangements so quickly to help with the transfer to witness protection."

"Kelan was thrilled to help. I think he's over trudging through the wilderness looking for escaped convicts." Walker smiled good-naturedly. "He also suggested the abandoned mine outside of Bison Valley."

"Why don't I remember that?"

"It's at the far edge, near town but not in Bison Valley," Walker reminded her.

Lizzie recalled the location. "Great idea." She messaged the information to Emmett, and he agreed to recon the place and get back to her.

When Emmett called an hour later, Lizzie and Walker were ready. Lizzie contacted Dex and gave him the details.

"If you're late, I won't hang around," Dex threatened.

"I won't be," she assured.

By the time they'd prepared to leave, Lizzie was crawling out of her skin. "I want to get this over with."

"Lizzie, please be careful."

"No worries about that. Plus, you all will be in the shadows watching." Lizzie slid her gun into her holster. "I learned my lesson about leaving the house without it," she half joked.

"We'll be close, but—"

She lifted her hand. "It'll take you a little while to reach me. This will work," she reassured him—and herself.

They left the residence in separate vehicles courtesy of Vandeaux, who'd delivered Lizzie's SUV to the safe house hours before, including the wire she'd wear to capture the meeting.

She trailed behind Walker's SUV, and they met Kelan on a less-traveled country road. Walker and Lizzie exited their vehicles. "Stay, Reena." Lizzie left the engine and air conditioner running.

Kelan approached them. "Ready?"

"Yes, the last thirty minutes has been excruciating," Lizzie replied.

"Okay, just to recap, once you've made contact and have the info, give the signal and we'll close in," Kelan said. "I'll take Dex into custody, so it appears as though I'm arresting him to divert suspicion should his cohorts see us. I'll transport him to the WitSec location."

"Thank you for assisting the task force with this," Lizzie said.

"Hey, my pleasure," Kelan said. "We're all in the same fight." He returned to his vehicle and headed out. They didn't want to garner attention by caravanning to the site.

"Are you certain about this?" Worry creased Walker's forehead.

She placed a hand on his forearm, feeling the muscles draw taut beneath her fingertips. "Definitely."

They climbed into their vehicles and set off, Walker lagging.

When they got closer to the location, Walker took a side road while Lizzie proceeded straight for the abandoned mine. Walker and Kelan would monitor her from a distance. They'd maintain the closest proximity and be her first line of backup.

She parked in front of the mine and, for a moment, second-guessed whether she'd made the correct decision.

Her phone rang. Emmett. "Lizzie, we're in place. Trevor is

positioned to your right and Eli to your left. We've got eyes three hundred and sixty degrees."

A flicker of relief coursed through Lizzie, but her nervousness overrode it. "Roger that. Should be here at twenty hundred." She referenced 8:00 p.m. military time.

Lizzie left the engine and air conditioner running for Reena, who panted quietly beside her. "It's okay, girl, we're getting closer to taking down this adoption ring and finding Mia." She stroked the dog's soft fur, immediately feeling calmer while she watched for any approaching vehicles. When Lizzie's dashboard clock read 8:45, she radioed in. "Maybe he's delayed."

"I hope so," Emmett replied.

By 9:30 p.m., Lizzie admitted something was amiss. She called and texted Dex, but he never replied. "I don't know what happened," Lizzie radioed to her team. "This isn't right."

"Keep trying to get ahold of him. We'll wait another hour," Emmett stated.

Lizzie dialed Dex's number again and tried four more times, but he didn't respond. Dex had seemed willing to talk and eager for the payout, so why the no-show?

"Lizzie, we're calling it," Emmett said.

"Okay." Lizzie shifted gears and drove off the property, spotting Walker's vehicle ahead of her and Trevor behind her once she was on the main road. She scanned her mind. They'd used burner phones to avoid detection of the call. So, who had knowledge of the conversation with Dex? Had he told someone? Fear for the CI coursed through her. Had Trigger gotten to Dex first?

When Lizzie and Walker returned to the safe house, she connected with the team via video. "We're back at the house," she said.

Emmett nodded. "Good."

"I'm worried for Dex," Lizzie began. "He's never pulled a no-show on me, and if Trigger got to him first—"

"Yeah," Trevor replied. "That means Trigger's hands reach farther than they anticipated."

"How's that possible?" Lizzie asked.

"Maybe the CI blabbed about the deal, and it got back to Trigger?" Emmett asked.

"I'll drive to Dex's favorite hangouts and check his apartment," Lizzie said.

"Negative," Emmett countered. "We'll take care of that, you stay put."

"Lizzie, send me the information," Trevor said.

Frustrated to be left out, she quickly typed the addresses and business names of the places Dex frequented.

"We'll split the list and get back to you," Trevor said.

"We'll be in touch," Emmett replied, ending the video call.

Lizzie and Walker called the local hospitals to see if any patients matching Dex's description had been brought in but came up with nothing.

"Get some rest," Walker said. "It's late, and we can't predict if we'll get called out again."

He was right, though she hated to admit it. They parted and headed to bed.

Lizzie was awakened by her cell phone at midnight. Trevor's information appeared on the screen, and she swiped to answer, "Hey," Trevor said.

A rap on her door and Lizzie sat up and flicked on the light. "Hold on, Trevor. Come in."

Walker entered and paused in the doorway.

"Walker's here, so I'm putting you on speakerphone."

"Sorry, Lizzie…but officers found Dex dead behind a Denver grocery store."

Lizzie bolted upright and gasped. "No."

"Emmett wanted to inform you."

She squeaked out, "Thank you," then disconnected before allowing her tears to fall.

Walker was at her side immediately, embracing her in his strong arms.

"It's all my fault. I killed him."

"This isn't on you. It remains unknown how Trigger, or the killer, located him."

"I shouldn't have pushed him to tell me anything." Reena jumped up beside her, placing her head in Lizzie's lap. "He was scared. I didn't listen or care. I was focused on the case and risked his life."

"Lizzie, you were unaware."

"But it's my job to protect my informants."

Walker stroked her hair. "You did the best you could. We couldn't compromise your safety after the kidnapping. You must think of yourself, too."

"There's no time for me to do that with a teenaged girl still missing and now Dex is dead!" Lizzie cried. She closed her eyes, feeling the weight of the news.

"You couldn't control what happened to him," Walker said.

"Do you really believe that?" Lizzie asked.

"Yes."

She blinked, an epiphany hitting her. "The same is true that you were powerless to prevent my abductions. You've done nothing but beat yourself up about it all. It wasn't your fault."

Walker blinked. "Thank you for that." He squeezed her.

His touch reassured her, and gratitude filled Lizzie. She couldn't imagine dealing with all they had without Walker. She glanced up, meeting his eyes. Her gaze traveled the length of his jaw. He oozed strength and confidence. Walker's touch grounded her, and the scent of his aftershave enticed her. Lizzie longed to tell him how she felt. How her feelings had shifted from a high school crush to a depth she'd never known before. He cleared his throat, and like a splash of cold water to her brain, Lizzie realized she had to stop thinking about Walker that way.

She pushed back, resolved to keep her head in the game. "We

can't change the outcome of what's happened with the baby smuggling case, but I'll ensure we double down on catching the escapees once and for all. Enough is enough."

NINE

The aroma of coffee wafted to Lizzie from her mug. She wrapped her hands around the cup and leaned back in her chair, positioned at a conference table in the Denver FBI building. Most of the task force had assembled for the emergency meeting to discuss Dex. Autumn and River were next to her.

Walker had been allowed to accompany her and was waiting outside the conference room. Maren and Eli entered and took seats across from them. Trevor and Melody videoed in.

Emmett occupied the head of the table. "Thank you all for coming on short notice," he began. "As you're already aware, Lizzie's confidential informant didn't show up for our meeting yesterday and was later found dead." He turned to Lizzie and offered a slight nod, acknowledging she should continue.

"Dex expressed fear regarding Trigger's real name and information. He adamantly refused to speak of it over the phone." Lizzie paused, gaining the courage to finish. She appreciated the compassion that filled her teammates' eyes. "I pressed him for justification for the in-person meeting, as well as his demands for financial provision, protection and relocation."

Lizzie's voice hitched. Autumn gave her hand an encouraging squeeze. "We're assuming his killer discovered Dex had communicated with us and silenced him. I take full responsibility for his demise."

"Lizzie, nobody blames you for what happened," Emmett reassured her. "We did our best to satisfy Dex's requests."

The plaguing guilt remained lodged in her throat despite her supervisor's kindness.

"I personally met with Dex's ex-girlfriend early this morning," Emmett said, gaining Lizzie's full attention. "That's why I requested this emergency meeting. Needless to say, she's distraught to hear of his passing."

Emmett's update was news to Lizzie. Why hadn't he talked to her about it?

"*Ex*-girlfriend?" Eli asked.

"Apparently Dex dumped her a month ago, though she didn't offer details," Emmett replied.

"Did she have any information that might help us?" Trevor inquired.

"She claimed to have no knowledge of Dex's arrangement with us, especially because he knew of Trigger's retaliation propensity."

Autumn leaned in. "Can she identify Trigger?"

That was the question they all wanted the answer to, and a hush filled the room, all eyes on Emmett.

"No." Emmett shook his head. "And based on her reaction to his name, even if she could, I'm doubtful she'd tell me."

Lizzie averted her eyes and stared a little too hard at the wood grain of the table. Again, that twinge of guilt niggled her. She'd pushed relentlessly, fearing for her own protection while encouraging Dex to trust her. How had she been so foolish?

"Lizzie, one of your superpowers is the ability to get informants and witnesses to talk to you," Emmett said. "You did a great job."

Lizzie dipped her head, silently arguing with her boss. If only she believed him.

"Dex's girlfriend said his eagerness for a payout was one of the reasons they fought so much," Emmett added. "He failed to consider the consequences of his actions. She mentioned a friend of Dex was a low-level worker for Trigger." Emmett raised a hand. "And before you ask, no, she didn't tell me his name."

A collective groan filled the room.

"Here's an interesting piece, though," Emmett said, regaining everyone's attention. "Dex told her that Trigger holds a master's degree in social work."

The group went silent at the news until Lizzie asked, "The leader of the adoption ring is a social worker?"

Trevor quirked a brow. "Motivated by a past incident at his workplace?"

"Or an encounter he had with an adoption agency?" Eli asked.

Melody inserted, "That can't be a coincidence."

"Agreed," Emmett said. "And if Trigger suspects we're on to him, he'll evade us."

"All the more reason we need to find him fast," Lizzie said.

The team's mutual agreement filled the space.

"Any word on the contenders for the lead K-9 trainer job?" River asked. The lead trainer of the training facility Dodger helped fund, Dev, was retiring soon, and everyone on the team was interested in who would take the job.

"No. And none of the candidates were successful in getting Trooper to follow more than a couple of commands," Emmett stated. "The puppies remain in training, but Trooper isn't progressing."

"Aw, that's disappointing," Lizzie responded.

"True, but even Dev wasn't able to get Trooper to obey commands," River added. The German shepherd was in training with his brother Chance, who'd so far excelled in K-9 work. The team was hoping Trooper would pull through, too.

"True," Lizzie agreed. "When Eli and I stopped by there last month, Trooper wasn't following a single command," she reminded the group.

"Maybe he's stubborn?" Trevor asked.

"That's possible, but it's a problem," Emmett said. "On the other hand, Chance is progressing very quickly and has shown a particular aptitude when paired with trainer Tanya Fielding."

Curiosity had Lizzie contemplating whether Tanya would get the job over Emmett's cousin Christian Dane. Surely the connection gave him an advantage. "You're rooting for Christian, right, Emmett?" Lizzie's cheeks warmed at the blurted inquiry.

Emmett shrugged. "I trust that's a decision best made by Dev and Dodger. It's fair to say the three of us have a stake in it, however, I have full confidence that the most qualified person will be selected."

What else could Emmett say? Lizzie secretly hoped Christian won the position. She wasn't close to Emmett and didn't know a lot about his life, but she sensed it would mean a lot for the solitary leader to be closer with a relative. Then again, Tanya knew Dev, a connection that would no doubt help her. And the third candidate, Jacob Wexley, was a family friend of Dodger's. She'd met Wexley and found him to be a bit pompous, though she liked Tanya and Christian. Any of them had a strong chance of getting the position.

Emmett concluded the meeting, and the team dispersed. Lizzie hurried to her rig, where Reena and Walker strolled the sidewalk. "She's a little antsy," Walker said. "How'd it go?"

She slid behind the wheel. "Hop in and I'll give you the scoop."

On the ride back, Lizzie shared what they'd learned about Dex. "But we have a mission to deal with right now," she said as she pulled onto the property of the safe house.

"Definitely," Walker said. "Let's find a way to trap the last escapees."

"Until we do that, I can't reason why or how they want me and are happy to kill you," Lizzie said.

"The only one that makes sense is Gregory Juhl wanting revenge on me," Walker replied.

"Putting him away doesn't explain why they're coming after me," Lizzie said.

A look passed over Walker's expression that Lizzie couldn't decipher. They exited the vehicle and headed inside, settling at the dining table. Walker removed his laptop from his bag and pulled up mug shots of Gregory Juhl, Vance Herrera and Anthony Arnold.

Lizzie's gaze flicked to the screen, then to Walker's hand, settled beside the keyboard. A flash through her mind made her gasp.

"What's wrong?"

"With the trauma of being kidnapped and drugged, I didn't remember this until now. Your hand movement triggered a memory."

Walker lifted his hand, studying it, then scooted closer, wafting a woodsy cologne her direction and momentarily causing Lizzie to lose focus.

"The man who abducted me had a weird tattoo next to a mole on his hand."

"Define weird."

Lizzie blinked, trying to recall the image. "Um, I think it was like a barb…no…a fishhook!" Excitement built as the details returned.

"Okay." Walker typed the data into a program that documented body art on inmates. "The escapees had plenty of tattoos at the time of incarceration, but none matching your description."

"But they must." Lizzie huffed. "Maybe they acquired it during their imprisonment—that's not unusual."

"True, however, the prison personnel update the system periodically. It's an important way to classify any gangs or affiliations the inmate has."

"If not them, then who else is behind this?"

"Something's off." Walker exhaled and started typing again.

"What're you thinking?"

"Let's expand the search perimeters in IAFIS."

Lizzie watched as he accessed the FBI's Integrated Automated Fingerprint Identification System, the national database comprised of criminal history data submitted by law enforcement. He narrowed the quest for a hook-shaped inking. "There're a few." Walker turned the laptop to face Lizzie. "Scroll through them and see if any are familiar."

Lizzie scoured the pictures, finally pausing on the third page of tattoos. She zoomed in to ensure it was the same image. "Yep, this is it."

Walker pressed a few keys to expand details on the bearer. Lizzie gasped. "What? No." Her heart stuttered, and she backed up her chair, nearly toppling it as she jumped to her feet. "It's not possible." She shook her head. "Are you sure? There's no one else?"

Walker glanced at the screen and did a double take, then looked again at the evidence board they'd worked on. "He's dead."

"Eddie Waterhouse was listed among the deceased." Lizzie pressed a hand against her chest. "Wasn't he?"

"Let's confirm." Walker called the prison warden and requested verification of the identities for those involved in the ambush. "Thank you." He disconnected. "He promised to personally verify the individuals and call back."

"That's not something they mistake. We're talking about death notifications made to families." Lizzie paced the room, replaying her abductions. "His voice—" She met Walker's eyes, then looked past him. The image of the liquor store shooting bounced to the forefront of her mind with Eddie Waterhouse's words ricocheting. *"You killed Momma!"* Lizzie sucked in a breath, her ribs still achy, and stumbled back.

Walker rushed to her side.

"Eddie!" Lizzie grasped both of Walker's shoulders, holding on for dear life. "At the cabin! How's that possible?"

"For now, let's suspend how Eddie's alive. Why target you?"

Lizzie's stomach roiled. "He vowed revenge at the shooting. Surely he heard Zeke shot Jennifer, not me."

"Revenge for the shooting makes sense," Walker said.

Lizzie gasped. "What if Zeke's in danger?" She grasped her phone and called her ex-boyfriend. A robotic voice replied the line was disconnected or no longer in service. "He must've changed his number."

"I'll try contacting his employer. Where'd he work after he left Littleton PD?"

"I don't know. We fell out of touch." Lizzie resumed pacing as worry for Zeke filled her mind.

Walker grabbed his cell phone and Lizzie listened as he placed a call asking for Zeke's last known address. He scribbled on a piece of paper and disconnected. "Here's the LKA."

Lizzie rushed to his side, then groaned. "That's old. He moved after he resigned from the department. There's nothing else available?"

Walker shook his head.

"What if Eddie already got to Zeke?"

"Don't panic, I'll call in the information on Zeke. He didn't disappear. We'll find him."

Lizzie dialed Eva Gomez.

"Hey, Lizzie."

"I'm sorry to bother you, Eva, but I really need your help."

"Sure."

"This isn't related to the investigation, but it is for the prison escapee case," Lizzie explained.

"Not a problem—Emmett said you might request assistance."

"Can you pull up everything on Eddie Waterhouse, including connections to girlfriends or other associates and his visitors in prison?"

"Yes. Give me a little time. I'll be in touch."

They disconnected and Walker's line rang. He answered, then gestured for Lizzie to move closer. "I'd like to put you on speakerphone with Officer Lizzie Reynolds." He nodded and set the phone between them. "Go ahead."

"I don't know how this happened," the warden began, "but my second in command advised the person wearing Eddie Waterhouse's wristband was Vance Herrera. Today, he received an anonymous call advising us to double-check Herrera's wristbands to his DNA on file. Again, I'd have notified you sooner but just learned about it."

A million questions tumbled in Lizzie's mind, but she didn't want to offend the warden. Based on Walker's expression, he had the same thoughts.

"He swapped the wristbands when he escaped?" Walker confirmed.

"Appears so." The warden sighed. "This is extremely embarrassing and there's no excuse. Although, in our defense, Mr. Herrera's face was mangled. I apologize for the misinformation, and I assure you I've initiated a thorough internal investigation."

"Warden, any idea who made the anonymous call?" Lizzie pressed.

"No, they used a burner phone and left it on my second in command's office voice mail."

"Can you confirm whether Eddie had a tattoo of a fishhook on his hand?"

"Let me check."

Lizzie nibbled on her fingernail until the warden returned. "Our files show the tattoo."

"Did Vance Herrera have a fishhook tattoo?" Walker asked.

"Not to my knowledge, however, his hands and arms were completely covered in ink," the warden replied.

It didn't matter. Vance Herrera was dead and couldn't be her kidnapper. Lizzie processed the information. Zeke was unreachable, and she feared the worst for him. Eddie's revenge threats were legit. He clearly wanted them dead badly enough that he'd planned the ambush. He wanted to inflict the damage himself rather than orchestrate a hit. Her vision blurred. But how had Eddie discovered her home address?

"Is there anything remarkable about Eddie, or people he associated with?" Walker asked.

"Eddie was a loner and got into a lot of fights," the warden said. "He was sent to the infirmary several times prior to the transport."

"For what?" Lizzie asked.

"Stitches, broken ribs and various contusions and lacerations." The warden sighed. "We do our best, but prison fights are common."

"Please send over his medical documents," Walker said and provided his email address.

"You got it. Sending now," the warden replied.

Lizzie's mind whirled. The death of his mother had devastated Eddie. He'd been inconsolable. "Warden, what's your understanding of Eddie's relationship with his father, Otho Mace?" Lizzie blurted.

"Otho was incarcerated in a different facility located in Sterling, so I can't speak to much of his life. It's illegal for inmates to interact without permission," the warden said. "We monitor all correspondence and communications. If contraband like cell phones are discovered, the offender is disciplined." Keyboard taps filled the line. "Eddie had two burner phones over the course of his incarceration. And he requested to speak with Otho, but it was denied."

"He was desperate to talk to his father before he died." Walker opened the message from the warden and turned his laptop to face Lizzie. They scanned the document. "The same nurse signed off on Eddie's treatment. S. Boyer—we should speak with her."

"Yes, Sierra Boyer is our in-house nurse," the warden said. "She's been on leave since the prison bus ambush where her brother, Miller, was killed."

"Miller Boyer the corrections officer?" Walker clarified.

"Yes. Tragic," the warden replied. "Sierra took it hard."

"Thank you for all your help," Walker said.

"You're welcome."

They disconnected and Walker said, "I think Sierra Boyer is

working with Eddie." Walker lifted a palm. "Hear me out. She had access to injectable drugs and an accomplice on the bus."

"Whoa. Just because her brother was on the bus doesn't make him an accomplice to the ambush."

"Maybe not, but that's hardly a coincidence."

Lizzie considered his idea. "I can't deny the connection with the drugs, though."

"Yep. And it's possible she left the anonymous message. If she was with him at the cabin, maybe she's seeking an escape from him. She didn't want to hurt you. Not to mention she's on leave, which she disguised at first as bereavement about her brother."

"I remember seeing her distraught at the command post," Lizzie contended. "I don't think she was acting."

"Fair. Things might've gone wrong," Walker said. "We can't underestimate her, though. If she's not the one who left the voice mail, she might be a willing accomplice helping Eddie to finish the revenge mission."

"Can't argue that. It's conceivable she stayed close to the investigation to apprise Eddie of updates."

"Makes sense to me. We need to talk to her, and fast. I'll ask Kelan to bring her in." Walker typed out a quick text.

Lizzie paced the area. "Jennifer, Eddie's mother, was a mess, involved with low-life bikers and petty crimes. Not to mention, she was married to Otho Mace, and his rap sheet was as lengthy as *War and Peace*."

"With different last names, it seems Otho was Eddie's stepfather," Walker said.

"Actually, Waterhouse was Jennifer's maiden name." Lizzie considered his question. "Eddie and Otho were tight, which was part of the reason they were sent to different prisons."

"Remember, Otho died about eight months ago, after a fight with a rival biker gang member," Walker said.

"Which explains Eddie's behavior trigger."

Walker glanced at an incoming text. "Kelan says he's on it."

Lizzie rose and poured fresh water for Reena. "I can't believe Eddie hates me that much. I mean, I get it. He believes I killed his mom. Until he stops trying to murder me, there's no way to reason with him."

"What worries me is how Eddie found you," Walker mused.

"Yeah." Lizzie swallowed hard. "I haven't a clue."

"And how do we catch him?"

Walker paced his room in the safe house staring at the text message from Kelan that had awakened him at one o'clock in the morning and left him concerned and confused. Need help ASAP! GSW to the L arm. Hurry! EW + ACC have me pinned at GOG. Dangerous. Don't bring cavalry, they'll run. Hiding 3G.

Walker unraveled the message, surmising EW was Eddie Waterhouse and ACC his accomplice. Kelan had a gunshot wound to his left arm. GOG meant Garden of the Gods Park, and he recognized 3G as the Three Graces formation. If Kelan was hiding and feared Eddie would hear him, it explained why he'd texted and refused to answer Walker's multiple return calls. And it was clear Kelan needed help and fast.

He couldn't leave without notifying Lizzie or having someone else stay with her. Walker contemplated waking Lizzie to accompany him, but if this was a trap, he couldn't risk her getting hurt or worse. Trevor Slate came to mind, and Walker resolved to ask him. Requesting backup to stay at the location wasn't feasible, because the safe house was confidential and they needed to keep the in-the-know people to a minimum. If Kelan had found something that he didn't want Walker to share, did it involve a fellow DUSM? If that were true, he had to notify Vandeaux. Walker trusted his boss implicitly and withholding intel was career death.

Walker called Vandeaux, but the line went to voice mail. At the late hour, perhaps he was asleep and not heard his phone. "Hey, boss, it's Walker. Got a cryptic message from Kelan. Says he's injured and Eddie Waterhouse shot him. Something's off.

I'm headed to check on him. Will have Trevor Slate assist with protective detail for Lizzie."

Walker called Trevor, who answered on the second ring sounding gravelly. "Hello."

"Hey, man, sorry to call at this hour, but I need your help."

"Sure, what's up?"

"I can't tell you everything, but can you come to the safe house and stay with Lizzie?"

"Sure. Give me the address. I'm on my way."

Walker appreciated that Trevor didn't pry for details. He relayed the location, and Trevor assured him he'd be there ASAP.

The late text added to the mystery of Kelan's communication. Why was he out at this time of night? Clearly, he'd not felt comfortable contacting Walker earlier via normal means. Had he discovered something about the case and decided to investigate on his own? An insider on the marshals or on Lizzie's agency? That would explain how the kidnapper had easily found her.

Walker rubbed his eyes and glanced at his watch. He needed to get on the road. He hadn't slept and couldn't shake the unease he felt about Lizzie's abduction and the deception Eddie Waterhouse had concocted. Why go through so much trouble to find Lizzie, but not kill her? What did the criminal have in mind? His cell phone chimed with a text and Walker glanced again at the screen at the message from Kelan. One word.

Hurry!

Walker couldn't wait. If the messages were legit, Kelan needed his help. The manhunt had produced no results and the more time that passed, the more the team feared Eddie had crossed the border. The problem was into which state—nobody had a clue. Colorado bordered Utah, Wyoming, New Mexico and Kansas. That left a lot of ground to cover.

Walker crept out of his bedroom and down the hall. Lizzie's

bedroom door was shut, and Reena was inside with her. He prayed the dog didn't alert.

A text from Trevor chimed. ETA three minutes.

Trevor was close. He hated leaving Lizzie...but Kelan didn't have much time. He was in grave danger, and Eddie didn't know where Lizzie was at the new safe house. Must leave. Walker exited the house, praying Trevor would arrive soon, then drove without the headlights until he arrived at the main county road and headed south to Colorado Springs. When he reached the Garden of the Gods Park, he parked farther down, then hiked the rest of the way. He didn't use the paved path to the Three Graces rock formation but instead wove to the meeting location. A shadow of clouds passed over the moon. As if this situation weren't ominous enough. Footsteps crunching on the ground gained his attention and Walker turned in the direction of the sound. A click sent the hair on the back of his neck rising in visceral response.

The accompanying blast had Walker diving behind a boulder. He bolted through the gardens, dodging gunfire the entire way. Unable to see anything in the darkened area, Walker didn't return fire. Was the assailant wearing night-vision goggles?

Walker took an alternative route to his vehicle, and once he was certain it was safe, he climbed inside and sped from the park. He put considerable distance between himself and his attacker before pulling over to gather his thoughts.

Had Kelan set him up? Only Vandeaux, Trevor and Kelan had the address to the safe house and knew Walker and Lizzie hid there.

Terror gripped his heart in a vise.

Lizzie!

The text was a ruse to get him away from Lizzie. Had Trevor walked into an ambush?

Walker increased his speed, phone pressed against his ear as he called Lizzie and Trevor. Both lines rang to voice mail.

Of course they'd not answer.

Fear roiled through him. There was no doubt Eddie had a partner. Was Kelan working with him? Were Walker's initial suspicions about his friend valid?

His phone rang with Vandeaux's name. "Where are you?" his boss demanded without greeting.

Determined to put an end to the deadly game Eddie and Kelan or whoever had planned, Walker sped through a synopsis of the events leading to the meeting at Garden of the Gods. "Have you heard from Kelan?"

"No, but I'll follow up. First, why on earth did you think meeting Kelan in the middle of the night without backup was acceptable?" Anger hovered in Vandeaux's tone, and Walker winced. "I realize how this looks, but don't jump to conclusions. If Kelan sent the message and he's injured, we need to rescue him. I can't fathom he'd get involved in something nefarious, especially with the likes of a criminal like Eddie Waterhouse."

If only Walker agreed. His so-called best friend had betrayed him once before. As much as Walker wished he felt the same, he didn't. "Someone sent me that text with the intention of killing me."

"No argument there. Get back to Lizzie and report in ASAP."

They disconnected and Walker pushed the speed limit, frantic to return to the safe house. When he pulled into the driveway, he spotted Trevor's patrol unit. He didn't bother shutting off the engine before sprinting from his vehicle and bursting through the front door. "Lizzie!"

Trevor stood at the door, gun at the ready. "Wow, I almost shot you." He lowered the gun.

Lizzie hurried from the bedroom, Reena at her side. "What's wrong?"

"Are you okay?" Walker didn't hesitate to draw Lizzie into his arms and hold on tight.

"Of course, why?" Lizzie didn't push away, but she stood stiffly, arms at her sides.

Walker caught Trevor's curious glance and took the hint, releasing Lizzie, then, in rambling word vomit, explained what had happened.

"You believe Kelan's involved?"

"I don't want to." Walker blew out a long breath and raked his fingers through his hair. "But someone figured out how to contact me as Kelan, and Vandeaux can't get a hold of him."

"It's time to end this." Lizzie rushed to her room. "Give me five minutes to get ready."

Walker secured the premises, watching and fully anticipating a full-on attack that never came. When Lizzie returned, she opened her laptop. "It's time for reinforcements. I'll call the team."

"Wait." Walker placed a hand on her shoulder. "What're you thinking?"

"I'll be the bait. Let's draw him out. Get Eddie, Kelan, whoever is after me to stop being a coward hiding behind shadows and force him into the open. We'll set up a takedown with backup."

"But these things don't always go as planned," Trevor warned.

Lizzie's eyes clouded with understanding. Her teammate hadn't meant to hurt her, but they had to make a wise decision.

"He's right," Walker added. "The best-laid stings aren't always successful."

"These criminals are clearly a step ahead of us," Trevor said.

"I think we can agree I am fully aware of that after what happened to Dex," Lizzie said in a clipped tone tinged with lingering sorrow.

"If Eddie manages to abduct you again, you might not escape his clutches alive," Walker continued.

"But if we do nothing, how many more people might be hurt?"

Walker and Trevor had no response to that. Lizzie was the bravest woman Walker had ever met, and her willingness to put her life on the line to take down these criminals impressed and terrified him. Still, he couldn't bear to lose her again. His phone rang, interrupting the conversation. "It's Vandeaux." He answered, Lizzie beside him. "Hey, boss."

"Walker, there's been an incident."

At the words, his heart stuttered and through the blood pounding in his ears, he heard his boss explain. "The safe house where your father's residing was infiltrated. The officer guarding the home is currently in critical condition with a gunshot wound."

"My dad?" Walker asked over the enormous rock in his throat.

"He was abducted."

Walker slammed his hand against the kitchen counter, startling Reena, who rushed to Lizzie's side protectively. He mouthed *sorry* to her.

"The kidnapper demands that you personally deliver Lizzie to him if you want your father to live."

Walker paced the room, fury boiling inside of him. "I gotta think."

"I'm using every resource available to triangulate the caller's location."

"Give me the number."

"Negative. The kidnapper's note warned you can use it one time only. After that, he'll destroy the burner phone, and you'll never see your dad again."

Walker's imagination took him to places he didn't want to visit. He had to do this right the first time. There was no room for mistakes.

"It also explains how someone used Kelan's contact information to reach you. The DUSM on duty with your dad had Kelan plugged into his phone. It's not hard to use an app to mimic the number. Telemarketers do it." Vandeaux's explanation made sense and Walker felt like a complete jerk.

Walker rubbed the ache at the base of his skull. "Have you reached Kelan yet?"

"No. We're still trying."

They disconnected and Walker paused, placing both hands on the counter and leaning forward, eyes closed.

"Walker, please tell me what happened." Lizzie stood behind him, her fear palpable.

He'd worried about her and focused on catching the escapees, then beaten himself up when Lizzie was abducted. All the time he'd wasted blaming himself and assuming his dad was safe. How many ways might he fail at his job? The same career he'd once prided himself on and put first in his life over everything else. His misplaced priorities needed an immediate adjustment.

"Please, I want to help," Lizzie pressed.

Walker turned to face her. "Someone kidnapped my dad."

Lizzie gasped. "What's the ransom request?"

"You."

She blinked, then touched his arm with a light squeeze. "It's time to request reinforcements. I'll ask the task force for help."

"This isn't their job or their mission," Walker reasoned.

"We're all law enforcement, and every one of them understands what it means when someone strikes close to home."

Walker shook his head. "How can I ask that of them after losing you? Multiple times." As if he wanted to add that.

"Nobody, including me, blames you," Lizzie protested.

"Normally, I'd put up a bigger fight, but I gotta rescue my dad. I'll take all the support possible."

Walker conferenced in Vandeaux while Lizzie did the same with her team. The task force leader, Emmett, agreed they'd assist and together the group hatched a plan. With the whole crew on video call, Emmett explained the situation. "We must find a way to draw the kidnapper out from under his rock."

"I'll go," Lizzie volunteered. "I'm the one he wants."

"Eli and Wrangler will be our takedown primaries," Emmett said, then to Walker, "Wrangler is trained in suspect apprehension."

Walker nodded understanding. His pride bowed to the desperation whirling inside of him. Vandeaux chimed in, "Trevor, please meet up with my DUSMs and the Bison Valley PD officers for backup."

"Lizzie and Walker, attend the meeting per the kidnapper's demands, but we'll maintain eyes on Lizzie," Emmett said.

"The abductor's intentions toward Walker remain a mystery," Vandeaux added. "It appears Lizzie is the main target, however, this might go bad. Once he has Lizzie, there's no reason for him to keep Walker or Bill McCane alive—"

"We have one chance to do this right," Walker interpreted.

Once they'd confirmed the plan, a marshal ran the burner phone to Walker while Eva worked with Vandeaux to initiate a linked conference call that permitted him to record the conversation. The tech used an app that made it appear the call originated from the burner phone number. The kidnapper answered with a voice-modification device.

"I want proof of life," Walker said.

"One time only."

A shuffle, then Walker's dad spoke. "Walker?"

"Dad. Are you okay? Are you hurt?" Walker tried to maintain professionalism, but his fear oozed through the line, giving his captor the advantage he wanted.

"Bring Lizzie to me in one hour. There's a housing project south of Highway C470 and Titan Road. Meet me in the construction company trailer."

The line disconnected.

With the plan officially in motion, Lizzie and Walker drove to the location. She turned off the highway as a text appeared on the burner phone. Lizzie pulled over. "He's changing his position," she said, reading the text aloud. "He wants to meet at the abandoned mine near Bison Valley. Says he knows we have backup, and we'd better lose them. He also warned us to leave our cell phones behind on the highway as he's tracing the GPS."

"The same place Kelan suggested for the meeting with Dex."

Walker shook his head. Too many things were pointing to Kelan being dirty.

"Don't go there yet," Lizzie said as though reading his mind. "He says if we don't come alone, your dad dies."

"It might be a bluff," Walker said.

"Are you willing to risk that?" Lizzie pressed.

Walker dropped his head into his hands.

"If we don't tell our teams, we have no backup. Without our cell phones, they'll never locate us. If things go sideways, we're on our own."

"I know."

The reality smacked Walker between the eyes. There was no way he'd ask Lizzie to offer herself up to a killer and basically trade places with his father.

"We need to update our teams," Walker said.

"Absolutely not," Lizzie contended. "Walker, we have to rescue your dad."

"Not this way. We'll figure something else out."

Lizzie shook her head. "This is my choice, Walker. We entered law enforcement careers acknowledging that we're willingly putting our lives on the line every day. Your dad needs our help, and we're going to be there for him."

Walker scoured his mind for another scenario.

A second text chimed, and Lizzie glanced at the screen.

Walker sucked in a breath. "What did he say?"

She read from the device. "'Don't take too long. I'm watching.'"

TEN

Lizzie considered the options. Without involving COK9, they were essentially throwing themselves on the kidnapper's mercy. Then what? "We have no idea how many criminals are involved with this mess," she reasoned. "We might be outnumbered."

"True."

"We could surreptitiously notify Emmett, and we go ahead of them?"

"He could have cameras or others watching and working with him. If they see your team arrive—"

"They'll kill your dad," Lizzie concluded. They had no other choice. "I'm going in as bait. You'll cover me and we'll bring your dad out safely. We must try the rescue alone."

"Lizzie—"

"Walker, as much as I'd love to argue with you, we're kind of on a ticking clock here. So, let's save the argument for afterward and get to work."

Walker exhaled. "You're stubborn."

"Yep. You've saved my life more than once these past few days. It's my turn to help you."

Lizzie felt Walker's piercing look, and something shifted in his expression. She prayed she'd not signed her own death warrant. She slowed down, tossing out their cell phones, and merged onto the road, heading south toward the abandoned mine with the kidnapper's directions.

"Of course, he'd force us to take a route that wouldn't be easily followed," Walker grumbled.

The neglected street's rough gravel caused the SUV to slam

into potholes. Poor Reena slid around in her kennel. “I’m sorry, girl.” Lizzie reduced her speed to lessen the jarring.

They traveled beyond the main highway and into the wilderness. Mounds of earth rose and fell around them in places where the land had been mined years before. Tall trees and high grasses surrounded them, providing many hiding places for their assailant.

At last, Lizzie pulled up to the mine entrance. Every fiber of her was second-guessing her decision. Once they entered the cavernous monster’s mouth that waited to consume them, there’d be no turning back. Worse, COK9 and the marshals weren’t privy to their location. Without their cell phone GPS, Lizzie’s only hope was they’d notice she and Walker were missing and search for them. Their teams knew both had strong work ethics and she prayed Emmett would understand the demands made under duress.

Ninety-nine percent of her trusted God would show them what to do. One percent of her wondered if that was unrealistic. And all of her feared the outcome. Lizzie realized at that moment, she’d relied on her training, boss, coworkers, even Reena for her faith and protection, but truthfully, God alone was her defender. Her invincible army, as her grandfather used to say. Now, more than ever, she needed Him.

Lizzie glanced at Walker. He’d confessed regret at not protecting her. She’d assured him that she’d held nothing against him. Did she?

God had taken care of her and helped her to escape the clutches of the kidnapper on more than one occasion. She had to believe, however this played out, God would watch over them and Mr. McCane. Even if she died in the process. That was the risk she and Walker had willingly accepted working in law enforcement.

“What about Reena?” Walker asked.

Jolted from her contemplations, Lizzie considered the option. “Without knowing the conditions inside the cave, I don’t feel comfortable taking her. She's too large for me to carry if the ground is unstable or if we have to climb." Lizzie's stomach twisted into knots. She wasn't fearful of dark, confining spaces, but the combination wasn't inviting. She'd heard horror stories about mines collapsing and trapping people.

She swallowed down the swirling nausea. No. She could do this. "I'll confine Reena in my vehicle. It's temperature-controlled, and she's safer there than she would be if things go wrong in there." She hoped the team found them soon.

Reena whined, her eyes pleading with Lizzie as though she understood the gravity of the situation. "Sorry, girl, but this is one time I can't have you with me." She ruffled the dog's soft fur and buried her face in Reena's neck. If this was their final moment together, Lizzie wanted to ensure Reena understood how much she loved her.

Resolute, Lizzie activated the temperature controls and locked the door, walking away from the SUV without looking back.

They approached the entrance of the mine, the dank smell of dirt and old wood filling her senses.

"This doesn't look safe," Walker said.

"I'm guessing that's the point." They ducked inside and Lizzie swept the flashlight across the hollow space.

When they were in the depths, a man ordered, "Drop your guns."

Lizzie whipped around, bouncing the light off the stone walls.

"Do it now!" he bellowed, rage echoing in the cave.

Lizzie sucked in a breath. Mr. McCane stood with his wrists and ankles bound, gagged with duct tape covering his mouth. Lizzie involuntarily gasped for air, recalling how she'd felt under the same confines. Whoever was behind him shoved the older man forward, and he stumbled, trying to maintain his balance. Walker started for his dad.

"Stay where you are or he's dead."

Walker's jaw tightened and he shifted closer to Lizzie. The

assailant forced Mr. McCane to sit on a wooden chair. The poor man's eyes were wide with fear.

His kidnapper stepped back into the darkness and a shuffle to her left demanded Lizzie's attention. Her gaze swept the space, spotting two gun-wielding men blocking any escape. Both were shadowed by the mine's encroaching atmosphere and the lack of light.

Lizzie's flashlight illuminated the fishhook tattoo on one of the men's arms. He stepped forward into the beam, and she met Eddie Waterhouse's venomous glare. He'd aged a little, but she recognized him from the liquor store shootout.

Walker mumbled something under his breath and Lizzie flicked a glance at him, then took in the sight of the second gunman, who had also advanced.

"Zeke!" Lizzie said.

"Toss your guns and key fob to the ground now," Zeke ordered. "Don't make me ask twice."

Lizzie's hand shook as she obeyed his order.

Walker hesitated, then complied. Zeke snatched the items and rushed from the cave, returning a few seconds later. Lizzie swallowed hard. Had he hurt Reena? "Zeke, why are you doing this?"

Her ex glared at her with palpable hatred. A shiver trickled down her spine.

"Did you hurt Reena?" Lizzie asked.

Zeke offered a wordless sneer.

"I cared about you!" Lizzie cried. "I feared something bad had happened to you."

"Right." Zeke snorted. "You were so worried in your new job and perfect world after destroying my life with your streak of honesty!"

"You made your choices," Walker growled.

"Shut up!" Zeke aimed at Walker. "Poetic justice having you return, though. Revenge is so sweet, isn't it?"

"Yes, it is," Eddie said, gaining their attention. "Which is why the cops are coming for you."

Lizzie and Walker shared a confused glance just as Eddie fired twice. Zeke dropped to the ground, clutching his stomach. He cursed, gasping for air.

"Did you really think I'd let you get away with it?" Eddie asked. "You're as much at fault for killing Momma as she is. And you're both gonna pay."

Zeke sucked in a breath, then whipped his head up and returned fire.

Eddie dodged into the darkness and shot back.

Zeke fell silent.

Lizzie screamed, covering her mouth.

Walker scooted closer to her, speaking loudly at Eddie. "Zeke killed your mom."

Eddie looked at them, the gun still aimed in their direction. "I was there. Believe me, I understand exactly how it unfolded."

The dim light and Zeke's position made it impossible for Lizzie to visually assess whether he was alive. *How'd Zeke get involved with Eddie?*

Eddie smiled and shifted his stance, pointing his weapon at Mr. McCane. "Go ahead, Pop, tell them about it."

Walker swallowed hard and Lizzie blinked, trying to comprehend Eddie's words. "Inform your awesome number one son who I am."

He ripped off the gag and Mr. McCane sputtered and coughed. He inhaled so deeply it pained Lizzie. "Eddie is your half-brother," he stammered.

Walker's face paled and he took a full minute before speaking. "Dad, what're you talking about?" He stepped forward.

"No, baby bro," Eddie chastised in a singsong voice. "Stay right where you are."

"I don't understand," Walker said.

"It was an acc—" Mr. McCane started to say but stopped short by Eddie's gun pressed hard against his temple.

"Surely you weren't about to call me an accident," Eddie taunted.

"No. Of course not. I didn't mean that," Mr. McCane stuttered. "I was young, and it was before I met your mother, Walker." His eyes stayed on Walker as though pleading for mercy.

Lizzie's gaze bounced around the space. Zeke hadn't moved, Walker seemed shocked in place and Eddie sneered viciously.

"Dad," Walker said. The one word a plea and demand for answers.

"He and my momma were quite the couple, right?" Eddie grunted. "Oh no, that's right. I'm a one-night stand. You didn't care enough about Momma to stick around, did you?" He smacked Mr. McCane on the side of the head with the gun.

Walker stepped forward.

"Take one more step and I'll shoot him," Eddie warned. "Zeke over there killed my mother without a second thought. And you abandoned us." Eddie pressed the gun harder against Bill McCane's temple, causing the older man to wince. "Isn't that right, Pop?" He spat the name as though it tasted bad on his tongue. "He trotted through life with no concerns. Without providing for his son and then had a brand-new family."

"I had no idea," Mr. McCane cried. "Jenny never told me."

"Right." Eddie thrust his elbow into Mr. McCane's chest, causing him to lurch forward in pain.

"Please, Eddie, it's not too late," Lizzie pleaded. "Let's talk about this."

Eddie turned a homicidal glare her way. "It's a little past the time for talking. Isn't it funny, though? I was conceived in one night, Zeke and Lizzie killed my mom in one night, and the only father who cared about me died in prison in one night. Now in one night I'm holding everyone accountable."

He lifted the gun, aiming at Lizzie.

•

* * *

"Wait!" Walker hollered, stepping in front of Lizzie to shield her.

"Get out of the way." Eddie gestured to the right with the gun.

"Not yet. Not until I've said what I need to say."

"What, brother dear?" A sardonic smile spread across Eddie's lips, and his sarcastic tone added to Walker's fury. "What brilliant words of wisdom are you offering?"

A million thoughts tumbled around in Walker's brain, vying for his attention. His father had had a relationship that resulted in Eddie's birth. Though Dad had claimed the interlude happened before he'd met Walker's mother, snippets of recollections from his childhood tugged at Walker. He remembered his parents arguing in hushed tones late at night when they assumed he was asleep. Were their conflicts because of Jennifer Mace and Eddie? Walker relied on his instincts, and it had boded well for him in law enforcement. That had him contemplating whether his father was telling the truth. Moreover, if his mother was aware of Eddie and his father's lack of responsibility to Jennifer, was that the catalyst for her abandonment?

Walker's child heart longed for a viable explanation to the devastating loss that had left him with deep scars. He'd never denied how deeply her departure had affected him, but he'd blamed himself, assuming she left because of something he'd said or done or how he'd burdened her life. Now, for a moment, he wondered if there was more to the story.

Was she a runner, like Walker? He'd convinced himself walking away from confrontation meant he'd been the bigger man, but the truth was, he ran from problems. Instead of standing up to Zeke, he'd folded and fled to Nebraska. Looking at the man claiming to be his half-brother, Walker couldn't help but feel sorry for Eddie. He saw the hurting boy desperately longing for answers.

"Is it true?" Walker asked. "Are you really my brother?"

A shadow passed over Eddie's eyes, and a momentary flicker

of softness swept between the hatred etched in his expression. He lowered the gun slightly. "Why else would I be here? Since I learned the truth, I haven't thought of anything other than making you all pay."

"Why me and Lizzie, though?" Walker asked, determined to keep Eddie talking, delaying in hopes backup arrived. Though he reasoned Lizzie's team had no reason to follow them here, since they'd not shared their destination or kept their cell phones. He had to talk Eddie off his emotional ledge and disarm him. "I get why you're angry at Dad—" He deliberately used the familial term to focus Eddie on their father as a person. "But if he remained unaware of you—"

"Are you calling my mother a liar?" Eddie lifted the gun again, aiming at Walker.

"Not at all. She had her reasons. Who knows why women do the things they do." Walker felt Lizzie's stare on him, trusting she'd not hold the comment against him. "My mom walked out without a second glance or an explanation."

Eddie seemed to deliberate the revelation. "Maybe Pop here should own up to his part in ruining the lives of two kids and their mothers." He pressed the tip of the gun hard against Bill's temple.

Walker fisted his hands at his sides. He had to do something, quick. "Although—" Walker let the word hang in the air for a few seconds. "If he was unaware your mom was pregnant, then he didn't knowingly abandon you. Not like my mom did."

Eddie snorted. "Are we comparing our sad childhoods?"

"No, I—"

"Both of you, move next to dear old dad!" Eddie bellowed. "Slowly!"

Walker and Lizzie cautiously crossed the space, taking positions on either side of his dad. Eddie took several steps backward, creating distance while keeping the weapon trained on them the entire time.

"Our dad—" Walker swallowed the bitterness in referring to

him that way, but he wanted Eddie's buy-in to the conversation "—has never lied to me. You don't have to believe that, but at least give him a chance to explain."

"He's had ample opportunity," Eddie sneered.

"I'm not lying." The pain in his father's expression nearly undid Walker as he shook his head vehemently. "I had no idea Jenny was pregnant."

"You could shoot all of us and end this, but wouldn't you rather learn the answers you've always wanted?" Walker pressed. "I do! Now that I'm aware you're my brother, I have a hundred questions."

Eddie's expression softened slightly. Beside Walker, Lizzie shifted behind his father. He noticed the tape that bound him could be easily sliced through if she had a knife. Like the one in his ankle holster. Walker fixed his gaze on Eddie, but in his peripheral vision, detected Lizzie's hand moving to her side.

"What difference would it make? I'm a convicted felon thanks to her!" Eddie's attention transferred to Lizzie.

She stiffened beside Walker. "Your conviction came as a result of your participation in the liquor store robbery where Zeke shot your mom," Lizzie said.

"Yeah," Eddie growled.

"I'll tell you the truth about that night," Lizzie said. "Not what the report said, but what really happened before you were apprehended."

Eddie's posture deflated for a second, then he seemed to reconsider, straightening his stance. "My mother died at the hands of two dirty cops, that's all that matters."

Lizzie flicked a glance at Zeke, who lay unmoving. "No," she said. "Jennifer slammed the door into Zeke, knocking off his body camera. He entered the store alone and fired, killing Jennifer. I came in behind him and caught Zeke placing a gun in her hands. He said she dropped it, but I never believed that. I think Zeke's shot was reactionary, not intentional. He got scared and planted the gun to save himself."

Eddie shook his head. "Shut up," he mumbled.

"This is between us," Walker interjected. "You want revenge because you feel let down. So, let's talk, man to man." He stepped in front of his father and Lizzie, shielding both from Eddie.

"I'm done talking. I have waited months for this. You're not going to stop me!"

Walker took another step forward. He prayed she understood what he wanted her to do. Eddie kept the gun trained on him, obviously considering Walker the greater threat. He advanced one small step away from his dad and Lizzie, turning Eddie's attention to the throat of the cave.

"We need to hash this out. Once you kill me and Dad, the answers will forever remain a mystery," Walker pressed.

"Like what?" Eddie asked.

In Walker's peripheral vision, Lizzie shuffled his father toward the cavern entrance. She'd cut him free of the tape binding his ankles and wrists, confirming she too carried a knife. *Good job, Lizzie.*

Walker had to keep Eddie talking to give Lizzie time to escape. The old adage about creating a common enemy filtered to mind, sparking the idea.

"This explains so much," Walker said. "All these years I hated my mom for leaving me, but now I know it's my father's fault."

"How do you figure?" Skepticism hung in his voice.

"It makes sense. My dad didn't do right by you and your mom, and my mother must've resented him for it."

"How's that work?" Eddie asked. "She sees it's wrong, then turns around and does the same thing?"

"They fought all the time." Walker continued moving closer to the cavern's depths. Now Eddie's back faced the entrance.

Lizzie and his father scurried outside.

"I think she hated him for it," Walker said.

Eddie hesitated, and his grip on the gun seemed to lighten. It was now or never.

Walker lunged for Eddie and a shot echoed.

The blast behind Lizzie froze her in place. Walker! She turned, then caught another glimpse of Mr. McCane. She had to get him away from Eddie and fast.

She rushed Mr. McCane farther from the cave. "Go as far as you can." Why hadn't she grabbed her key fob from Zeke?

She didn't have time to argue with him or provide detailed information. They had to move him before Eddie killed him.

The older McCane opened his mouth to protest, then must've thought better of it and jogged in the direction of Lizzie's vehicle before turning and running the opposite way toward the road.

Lizzie returned to the cave, grateful to hear the men arguing louder. Had the gunshot been a warning or had the shooter missed?

She inched by the entrance, listening.

"Nothing ever goes my way!" Eddie complained. "But I'm taking what I want, and that starts here immediately!"

"You're a fugitive. There are tons of people searching for you. Even if you kill us, you won't escape," Walker argued.

Eddie spun to face her, catching Lizzie off guard. She gasped.

"Get in here now," he warned. "Where is my father?"

"He's gone."

Eddie cursed. "He's an old man and won't get far. It's time to finish this. Move toward your dying boyfriend."

Lizzie rushed to Walker's side. "Are you okay?"

"Don't worry about me. Get out of here," Walker whispered.

"Stop your murmuring!" Eddie bellowed, swinging the gun too quickly between her and Walker. "You're going to pay for what you did to my mom."

"I didn't kill her!" Lizzie protested.

"So you say. You're a liar." Something in Eddie's expression changed.

Without warning, Walker dived, grabbing Eddie's legs and yanking him to the ground. The gun toppled between Eddie's outstretched arms and Lizzie's legs. He kicked free of Walker's hold and lunged for the gun at the same time Lizzie did. Eddie reached it first, swinging it in her direction.

Walker threw himself in front of her just as the blast of a gun exploded a second time, deafening her.

Walker held Eddie down and ordered, "Go get help!"

Lizzie hesitated and Eddie wriggled from under Walker. The two battled, fists flying, arms and legs in a whirling tornado of punches and kicks.

"Go!" Walker commanded, restraining Eddie. Lizzie saw the crimson stain forming on Walker's shirt.

She gasped and hurried to where Zeke lay. She withdrew the key fob from his pocket and he groaned, confirming he was still alive. At least for now. Lizzie bolted outside. With one hand, she hit the button on the remote, releasing the kennel door. Reena bounded out and rushed to her side. Lizzie exhaled relief as she hurried to her unit and grabbed the burner cell phone. There was no way she'd leave Walker here alone, but she had to call for help. Lizzie tried dialing and noticed she had no signal. She slid into the driver's seat and tried to start the engine, but it didn't make a sound. She slammed her hands on the steering wheel. Of course, Zeke had disabled the vehicle when he'd rushed outside and smirked at her question regarding Reena's safety. He'd wanted her to worry about her dog.

"Your boyfriend's dead," Eddie taunted from inside the cave. "I'm coming for you."

Lizzie grabbed Reena's collar and rushed into the woods to hide. Where had Mr. McCane gone? She hoped he'd run as far away as possible. Eddie expected her to flee to the road, but instead she ventured deeper into the forest, seeking the shadows. Lizzie kept trying to call, but the phone didn't register reception.

"Don't make me chase you," Eddie taunted, his footfalls heavy on the pine needle–covered ground behind her.

Lizzie motioned for Reena, using hand signals to remind the dog to stay quiet as they crept farther into the woods.

"Hide," Lizzie whispered to Reena, reminding her of the game they played.

The dog's tail wagged in agreement. Though they'd just started the skill, Lizzie prayed Reena remembered how to do the reverse-tracking method since they'd only practiced it a handful of times. She shoved away the reminder that the last time they'd practiced, Reena had gotten bored and rushed out of their hiding spot.

Lizzie stumbled on a deep crevice where a creek or stream had once parted the earth. And the idea sprouted. If she got Eddie to step into the crevice, it would catch him off guard and she could disarm him from behind.

"Stay," Lizzie whispered. "Guard." Reena assumed the position. Though she wasn't an apprehension dog, she understood the command.

Lizzie gathered sticks and broken branches to cover the place. Then she moved to the left, where a large boulder faced the snare. She visually roved the area for another spot to hide and chose a cluster of bushes. Lastly, Lizzie forced impressions of her boots in the ground in all directions, intending to confuse Eddie. Satisfied with the trap she'd set, Lizzie pulled Reena behind the shrubbery, squatted and waited.

As expected, Eddie tromped through the woods, following her trail better than she'd anticipated. He turned in front of her, his boot right next to the trap. If he hesitated, the ground cover she'd planted might fall and give it away.

Come on. Lizzie silently willed Eddie to step forward.

At the last minute, Eddie spun on his heel, narrowly missing the snare. Lizzie bit her lip. She scooted back, accidentally stepping on a branch. It snapped, and Eddie turned her direction. She'd disclosed her hiding place.

She froze and he leaned over the bramble, locking eyes with her.

Reena growled and Lizzie swallowed hard. If she released her dog, Eddie would undoubtedly shoot Reena. They held their silent standoff for several seconds.

Lizzie started to rise when a loud whistle startled them both. Eddie stepped backward, searching for the sound, and his leg dropped into the trap.

He cursed and his knee buckled, forcing him down. Lizzie bounded from her hiding spot and tackled Eddie. His gun toppled to the earth, and she forced him down in an awkward bend. His foot was caught in the snare, making him unbalanced, and she tugged his arm behind him.

Footsteps approached from the path.

"Here!" Lizzie hollered.

"Get off me!" Eddie growled, trying to wrench free of her hold.

Reena emitted a low growl, stepping closer in a stalking stance. Eddie silenced.

Through the trees, Walker burst onto the scene, clutching his side. Crimson stains covered his shirt, and his face was screwed up in pain. Still, he'd come for her. Behind him, Eli and Trevor rushed to Lizzie.

Relief coursed through her as Walker jerked Eddie upright, snapping on handcuffs. He tugged him out of the crevice while Trevor reached down a hand to help Lizzie step up.

With Eddie in custody, Lizzie, Trevor and Walker headed back to the mine, where several other task force members waited with Kelan.

"How did you guys find us?" Lizzie asked.

Kelan gestured toward the back seat of his car. Lizzie stepped around him and spotted Sierra handcuffed. "Got her at the command post. She's been keeping close tabs on the investigation. Once I confronted her, she confessed her part in helping Eddie."

"Wow," Lizzie and Walker chorused.

Eli sat beside Zeke, who lay handcuffed with Wrangler standing guard intimidatingly by his side. Zeke didn't dare move or try to resist. He was conscious but clearly injured. The sound of sirens reverberated as rescue roared onto the scene. Eli moved Zeke toward the ambulance, where EMTs helped load him into the rig. Eli transferred the shackles to the stretcher, ensuring Zeke didn't make any escape attempts. They bandaged Walker's wound where the bullet had grazed his side.

Hurt or not, Lizzie had a lot of questions, and she wasn't waiting. She bolted for them. "Zeke, why?"

He blinked at her, then looked past Lizzie to where Trevor escorted Eddie toward a patrol unit. "He planned to frame me for everything," Zeke said.

Lizzie addressed Eli and the paramedics. "Please give us a minute."

They nodded and moved back, but Eli stayed close, weapon at the ready.

"Really, dude? What am I gonna do handcuffed to a stretcher?" Zeke glared at Eli.

Eli shrugged but didn't move.

"Whatever," Zeke mumbled then turned to Lizzie. "After what you did to me, you have the audacity to ask why?"

Walker stepped closer, and Lizzie raised a hand, asking for space, and shook her head. This was between her and Zeke. "You're still passing the blame."

"I wanted revenge after you took everything from me. You got all the recognition and career awards that belonged to me. You proceeded to find a better job, your career skyrocketed and you succeeded while I was permanently barred from law enforcement work. Explain how that's fair? We were on the same call, the same incident!"

"You chose to lie, Zeke. You shot Jennifer Mace and planted a gun on her."

"That's not what happened and you know it," Zeke argued.

Lizzie raised her hands. "I was there." She calmed her tone. "She startled you and you reacted. That would've been understandable. Jennifer was armed, so we have no idea whether she'd have opened fire on us. But you planted the gun and that changed everything. Own it!"

Zeke frowned and averted his eyes.

"I need to understand how you connected with Eddie and discovered Bill McCane was his biological father."

At the mention of his father's name, Walker stepped closer. "At least tell me that much," he added.

Zeke stared at him for a long time before replying. "After I lost my career—" he paused to glare at Lizzie "—I had to reinvent myself. What better way than to make some powerful friends in Otho Mace's rival biker gang? Met a nice lady there who had a crush on me. With a little convincing, she helped me by winning Otho's affections through letters and visits to prison, and I got intel on Eddie and Otho. I planned to have them killed, but imagine my shock when I learned from Otho's new girlfriend that Bill McCane was Eddie Waterhouse's real father. Amazing what folks will do for a little cash." Zeke laughed and launched into a coughing fit. Once he regained control, he continued, "I knew right then, I had everything I needed to get the revenge I wanted. It was like being handed a gift, perfectly designed and waiting for me."

"But you never expected Eddie would turn on you," Walker surmised.

Zeke shrugged. "Should've foreseen it. There's no honor among convicts. Eddie got what he wanted and had no reason to keep me around, especially if he planned to escape again."

"Why? What you did to Lizzie was unconscionable, but I at

least understand why you wanted revenge. What did my dad and I do to you?" Walker asked.

"Dude, you don't get it, do you?" Zeke seemed to study him. "Always the big innocent hero act." He exhaled loudly. "In high school you had all the girls' attention."

Walker did a double take. "Lizzie was the only girl I ever asked out, but you managed to sabotage that."

"That was the whole reason. I finally wanted to show you what it felt like to be passed over." Zeke snorted. "Yeah, well, you can see that was worthwhile."

Lizzie scowled at him. "What about Eddie's involvement in this?"

"I guess if I'm going down, there's no point in withholding anything. I'm familiar with how this goes. First, you promise you'll tell them how I cooperated."

It was irrelevant. Zeke was a trained law enforcement officer, even if he didn't work in that capacity anymore. The courts wouldn't have a lot of compassion for him.

"Sure," Lizzie blurted. "What about the woman working with Eddie?"

Zeke laughed. "Oh yeah. He turned on the charm and conned the prison nurse, Sierra Boyer, into helping him. What a doorknob. He promised her a huge payout, which of course he couldn't deliver. He even convinced her to drag her brother into the ambush. Genius."

"He was killed," Lizzie said.

"Yep. Cost of doing business." Zeke laughed.

Lizzie stared at her former boyfriend. When had he grown so cold and callous? "For what it's worth, Zeke, I'm sad things ended as they did. But I'm not sorry for telling the truth."

Zeke snorted. "Whatever." He flicked his hand the best he could with the handcuffs restraining him. "Let's go. I'm done talking." He turned his head, and Lizzie and Walker stepped away.

"Give me a second," Lizzie said, approaching Trevor.

"Sure." Walker retreated, giving her room.

"Thank you for coming to my rescue," she said to Trevor.

He smiled shyly. "Thank Mr. McCane. He had a cell phone tucked in his pants pocket. When he reached the road, he called 911. It was a long shot, but since Kelan's 'message'—" he used his fingers to make air quotes "—mentioned this mine, we headed here once we lost your GPS."

"I know you've got a lot going on at home with your mom's care. Thank you for helping with all of this."

Trevor nodded.

"Everything okay with her?" Lizzie asked.

"It's not easy, but I'm working to find the best possible solution for her." Trevor sighed. "We're getting there one day at a time."

Lizzie didn't pry but placed a hand on his shoulder. "Seriously, if there's anything I can do to help or if you need an ear, I'm here."

"Thanks. I appreciate it."

"Guess we'd better debrief with the team." Lizzie led the way, and they approached the group. "Trevor told me how you found us. That was brilliant."

Lizzie explained how she'd gotten the text directing them to go to the abandoned mine instead. "We wanted to tell you, but Eddie threatened to kill Mr. McCane."

"It's on me."

"Walker—" Lizzie began.

"No, I own my mistakes," Walker said, touching her arm gently. "I was afraid he'd kill my dad, and I couldn't chance that. I made the decision, and I'm willing to accept the consequences."

Vandeaux shook his head. "I don't think that's necessary. Exigent circumstances."

Lizzie offered a small smile, grateful his boss wouldn't discipline him. "Reena performed the hide technique perfectly. She let me know where Eddie was, and we were able to set the trap." She stroked her dog's soft ears. "Shall we talk to Sierra?"

Walker provided a recap of what Zeke had told them about the nurse's involvement.

"Report in as soon as possible," Emmett said.

Walker and Lizzie headed to her SUV and slid behind the wheel after she'd loaded Reena. "Thank you for coming back for me."

"Are you kidding? The only thing I cared about was making sure you were okay." Walker touched her arm. "Lizzie, your selflessness in helping me rescue my dad…it was amazing. My feelings were already returning for you from the first second I saw you. But that…" Walker paused. "That was the final straw that made me fall for you again. I should've fought for you and explained myself in high school. We might've seen how deceitful and tricky Zeke was. Maybe then…" His voice trailed off.

Lizzie gaped at Walker's confession. "As much as I wish things had turned out differently back then, I'm more concerned about where we go from here."

A strange look passed over Walker's face, and he averted his gaze and didn't reply.

Lizzie's heart ratcheted in her chest and she realized he must not want the same. It was finally over—they'd caught Eddie and Zeke and had enough evidence that even without Sierra's testimony, both men faced a slew of charges. But none of it mattered because Walker had no intention of giving Lizzie a second chance.

"You said yourself you'd never date another LEO."

"I did, but—"

"I'm sorry, Lizzie, it's just best if we wrap up this case and go our separate ways." He turned his gaze out the window, leaving Lizzie confused and sad. The biggest takedown of her career, and though she should be elated, all she could think was that she'd somehow lost again.

ELEVEN

Walker and Lizzie peered through the interview window to where Sierra Boyer waited for them. “I can’t believe it was her the whole time.” Lizzie shook her head. “I never would’ve suspected.”

The pretty blonde wore a pink long-sleeved shirt and had the same fishhook image inked on the back of her right hand.

“I wonder if that was some kind of lovers’ pact,” Lizzie said, gesturing toward the tattoo.

As though sensing Lizzie’s comment, Sierra pulled down her sleeve, concealing it.

“She wasn’t incarcerated or arrested, so it wasn’t logged in the system,” Walker explained. “Is she responsible for attacking you?”

“No, it was definitely Eddie. He has a mole beside the tip of the fishhook,” Lizzie said.

It was the most she’d spoken to him since the arrest, and he was grateful they could at least work together. “Ready to interview her?” Walker asked.

“Yep.” Lizzie spun on her heel, and they entered the interrogation room. Sierra glanced up but didn’t appear surprised to see them. It was almost as if she’d resigned herself to her fate.

“Thanks for agreeing to meet with us,” Lizzie said, taking the closest seat with Walker beside her.

“Like I had a choice.” Sierra burst into tears. No one spoke for several seconds. “I’m sorry,” she said, gathering herself. “It’s just ironic.” She glanced down at the tattoo. “Eddie said we were hooked on each other, and I did everything he asked. I thought he loved me. Now my brother is dead and I’m going to prison. I guess no amount of book learning ever teaches wisdom, huh?" She met their eyes.

"Sierra, you seem levelheaded. How did you get involved with Eddie?" Walker asked.

She shrugged. "It didn't happen overnight. Eddie's sweet and thoughtful. He'd gotten beat up severely in prison and I was his nurse. I don't know. We started talking and he was cute. Shy and tender around me." She blinked, eyes welling with tears. "It was all an act, huh?" Sierra shook her head. "I'm so stupid."

"You are not," Lizzie reassured her. She thought of the missing pregnant teens and how that same type of thinking would endanger them and keep them imprisoned by their captors, believing they weren't good enough or deserved what they got. "Eddie is a manipulator. He played you, but that wasn't because you're unintelligent."

Sierra shrugged again. "I guess. I tried to fix it, even though it was too late."

"You were at the cabin," Lizzie said. "Thank you for helping me to escape."

Sierra nodded. "I tried to buy time and hoped you'd get outta there before Eddie returned. I knew they'd catch me. That's why I hung around the command post so much. Eddie sent me there, said I needed to monitor the manhunt, but he remained at the abandoned mine and the search party never considered that location."

"If you cooperate and testify against Zeke and Eddie, it might help you with the DA."

"And I'll tell them how you helped me at the cabin," Lizzie added.

"Ultimately, though, it's up to them how they want to prosecute," Walker explained.

"Okay." Sierra let out a long breath, a classic sign of her readiness to confess. "When Eddie and I got involved, he talked about getting out of prison. That's not uncommon and I didn't make too much of it. But as we got closer and he learned about his stepfather's death, he became obsessed. He shared his escape plan and said he needed someone on the inside to help with the prison bus ambush."

"You recruited your brother, Miller," Lizzie inserted.

"He didn't want to do it. My brother's a good man. Was a good man." Her lip quivered. "But when I told him that I'd aided Eddie, he worried I'd go to prison if Eddie ratted me out. He tried protecting me," Sierra said, her eyes welling with tears again. "Anyway, he orchestrated the ambush. Eddie set up the thugs on the outside. But I promised I wouldn't hurt anyone." Sierra looked down. "I guess that's a moot point now, huh? But I refused to kill you. Eddie figured Walker needed a little more incentive, and then the other guy—"

"Zeke?" Walker asked.

"Yes, he demanded you both be brought in alive. Honestly, that saved your life," Sierra said.

Lizzie disagreed, but she didn't comment.

"When I learned about Miller's death, I told Eddie I wanted out, but he threatened to kill me if I talked to the cops." Sierra swiped at her damp cheeks.

"What about the drugs used on Lizzie and Reena?" Walker asked.

Sierra hung her head. "Stolen from the prison pharmacy."

"Eddie lacked the medical knowledge to administer them," Lizzie said. "You helped."

Sierra bit her lip, and her silence spoke the truth. Her information filled in all remaining unclear points. Sierra would face conspiracy charges; that couldn't be helped. When they'd finished taking her statement, Walker and Lizzie exited the room and Vandeaux entered to finish the process.

"She's going to prison for a long time," Lizzie said.

Walker nodded. "Yeah, I guess one bad choice snowballed."

"We need to get back to headquarters for briefing. Kelan and

Vandeaux will meet us there." Lizzie led the way out of the building, not looking back. She longed to tell Walker of her heartbreak. Not about Zeke. He was a jerk; his revenge motivation and plan were equally ridiculous. But she'd anticipated that she and Walker would get a second chance. They'd both acquiesced to Zeke all those years ago—could they fight for each other now?

Walker exited the meeting with Kelan after her team debriefed. The marshals had captured the last two inmates, Gregory Juhl and Anthony Arnold, near the New Mexico border. Neither was involved with the ambush; they'd taken the opportunity to run.

Walker and Lizzie hadn't spoken much after the interview with Sierra, leaving palpable tension between them. Even with the huge success of finding and naming Eddie and Zeke in the crimes, the result left them disappointed. What joy would Lizzie have after learning the man she'd once loved had tried to kill her? His mind played the whole event on repeat, and though he didn't understand how Zeke's hatred for him had drilled so deep, he couldn't hold on to the resentment. The weight proved excessive, and Zeke's bitterness sufficed for everyone.

Walker wanted to confess to Lizzie how the entire case had played on his fear of being unable to keep her from harm. The bottom line was that at every opportunity, he'd failed to protect Lizzie. How could she love a man like him? And even if she ignored his shortcomings, he remained undeserving of her love. Add in the revelations about his dad and Eddie that threw him for a loop and ignited emotional numbness, and Walker felt even more closed off to a relationship. It was all a little too similar to the days after his mother left.

His father adamantly denied knowing about Eddie, and Walker believed him. Regardless, he loved his dad and wouldn't hold his past against him.

"Wanna grab something to eat?" Kelan asked.

"Sure." Walker slid beside Kelan in the SUV and his partner drove from the parking lot. "Hey, man, I owe you an apology."

"For what?"

"Lizzie and I go way back—" Walker began, not sure why he chose to start with that information.

"She's a special lady," Kelan agreed.

Walker swallowed down the rock on his throat. "She is, and she deserves the best. Zeke really threw her under the bus on the Waterhouse case. I can't imagine how furious she must be about all of that."

"Yeah, he's something else. Are you done playing hard to get?"

Walker blinked. "What?"

"Bro, you cannot be serious. It's blatantly obvious that you are smitten with Lizzie."

"Doesn't matter. She deserves someone who'll love her the right way."

"And you're not that guy?"

"I've got too much baggage."

"You and the rest of us. But if that's your reasoning, it's weak."

"I'm attracted to her, but it can't be more than that."

Kelan guffawed. "Notify Vandeaux you're not undercover material. I can see right through you. Seems to me, and granted, I only have part of the story, but you made a foolish decision to let her go the first time. Don't make the same mistake twice."

Walker grimaced. "It's not that easy."

"Why not?"

"I messed up. She needed me to protect her."

"Say what? Dude, did we meet the same Lizzie Reynolds? In my opinion, she's capable of protecting herself."

"Nah, you don't get it. How many times was she threatened?"

"I'm guessing about the same number of life-threatening situations you faced." Kelan shook his head. "It wasn't all on you or her to prevent it. You're not a superhero. Sometimes bad things happen to good people who don't deserve it. But God is the one in control, and His shoulders can carry those massive questions better than ours can. You want to fight for her? Do it now."

Walker considered his friend's words. "You really think she's into me?"

"If I have to draw you a picture I will, but you're supposed to be a trained observer."

"Maybe you're right." They exited the car and headed into the fast-food restaurant, but Walker's mind was a hundred miles away, working on what he'd say when he talked to Lizzie. "Hey, is it all right if we got this meal to go?"

Kelan laughed. "Took you long enough."

When Walker finally arrived at Lizzie's house, he stood on the porch step, searching for the right way to approach her. Kelan's words tumbled around in his mind. Lizzie had reached out, and he'd shot her down. What if she was done with him?

"You going to knock or just stand outside until the sun rises?" Lizzie asked, approaching from behind him. Reena sat next to her. "Saw you when we finished our walk."

"How long have you been watching me?" Heat coursed through Walker's face, making him grateful for the dark.

"Long enough." She released Reena and the dog trotted into the yard, sniffing happily.

"I, uh, wanted to come by and apologize."

"For what?"

"You tried to talk to me earlier and I shut down."

"Yeah," Lizzie said, leaning against the banister. "It's okay, I shouldn't have assumed anything. I suppose I'd picked up the same vibe from you, but clearly, I misjudged. Sorry for putting you in that position."

"No, you didn't misread me at all." Walker exhaled and dropped on to the chair on the porch. "Lizzie, I've been blaming myself for all the bad stuff that kept happening to you."

"Why? You aren't responsible for Zeke or Eddie's actions. Didn't we discuss that ad nauseam?"

"Right, but I felt accountable for not protecting you."

"Why?"

He shrugged. "When all the stuff happened in high school, I should've spoken up and fought harder for you. But my own insecurities got in the way, and I backed out, telling myself I was doing us both a favor. That Zeke was a better fit for you."

"Ha." Lizzie snorted. "Well, Zeke fooled us both with his lies. Walker, I've got comparable training as you. I'm perfectly capable of taking care of myself. But nobody can predict an ambush. You're off the hook for the attacks Eddie orchestrated."

Walker smiled. "Duly noted."

"As far as ducking and dodging any romance, whether it's with me or someone else, you're only hurting yourself. You have a lot to offer, and any woman would consider herself beyond blessed to have a relationship with you. But none of that matters if you believe you're undeserving. Let me put it another way. It's like having a present under the Christmas tree. It's got your name on it and it's obviously yours, but if you refuse to open and claim the gift, it's useless."

"My dad used a similar analogy to explain grace and forgiveness to me when I was a kid."

"Smart man," Lizzie replied. "By the way, how'd things go with him when you talked?"

Walker regarded her, recalling the conversation with his father. "He insists he knew nothing of Eddie but concedes Jennifer Mace reached out to him several times over the years. Thus creating tension with my mom. He learned about Jennifer's associations with biker gangs and refused to respond to her for fear she was trying to stir up drama."

"Wow, can you imagine if he had?" Lizzie shook her head.

"I can't help but wonder if Eddie's revenge would've been halted by one conversation between him and my dad."

"No, I think Eddie used that as a foundation, but realistically, he had deeper issues." Lizzie touched his arm gently.

"I don't blame my father. He recognizes he made a mistake and asked forgiveness."

"I agree. And he's dead-on accurate about accepting forgiveness and grace. If you refuse to accept the gifts freely given to you, nobody can force them on you."

Walker met her eyes and got to his feet. He took Lizzie's hands into his own. "Lizzie, no amount of time has diminished how crazy I am about you. I chickened out once, I won't do it again. I've been stubborn and foolish, but I don't want to be that way anymore." He regarded her intently. "I meant what I said. Your selflessness in helping rescue my dad confirmed what I already knew. I am in love with you. Always have been. Would you permit me one more opportunity to make you fall in love with me?"

Lizzie laughed, taking Walker aback. "Sorry, I'm not laughing at you. Walker McCane, I've had a crush on you since ninth grade. Your mission is already completed there. But I'd sure love to start fresh from here."

"Yes, please." Walker stepped forward, his gaze traveling the contours of her face.

Reena pushed between them, glancing up with expectation. Lizzie laughed. "Reena wants to make sure you're in it to win it," she teased.

Walker entwined one hand with Lizzie's, using the other to pet Reena. "I promise to do my best to show Lizzie how much I care."

Reena wagged her tail and strolled past them, lying on the porch.

"I guess that means she accepts your offer," Lizzie joked.

"I do get called out for work unexpectedly," Walker admitted.

"I can live with that."

Walker stepped closer, and Lizzie lifted her chin. He wrapped his arms around her waist, leaned down and pressed his lips against hers. A spark and the rush of attraction passed between them.

When they parted, she asked breathlessly, "You told me your career makes it hard to be in one place."

"It requires me to be gone a lot if I opt for certain assignments."

"Ah, a little caveat you left out."

He shrugged. "I can work from the Denver office and commute until we're married."

Lizzie blinked. "Now, that's confidence in our relationship."

"I let you go once. I'll never do that again." He smiled softly. "Is that a yes?"

Lizzie rose on her tiptoes and kissed him again. "What do you think?"

* * * * *

If you enjoyed this story,
don't miss Hunting an Arsonist,
the next book in the
Colorado K-9 Unit series!

Discover all the books in this brand-new continuity:

Searching for the Truth *by Laura Scott*
Tracking the Taken Child *by Sharon Dunn*
Danger in the Rockies *by Terri Reed*
Protecting the Baby *by Jodie Bailey*
Fugitive Manhunt *by Sharee Stover*
Hunting an Arsonist *by Jessica R. Patch*
Uncovering Explosive Secrets *by Maggie K. Black*
Unraveling a Crime Ring *by Valerie Hansen*
Christmas K-9 Security *by Lynette Eason & Lenora Worth*

Available only from Love Inspired Suspense!

Dear Reader,

I hope you enjoyed Walker, Lizzie and K-9 Reena's story. I'm a Colorado native, so it was a lot of fun for me to write about my hometown, where I could easily picture familiar places. I love second-chance stories, because our God specializes in them. Sometimes asking for a second chance is the scariest thing we can do. We wonder, what if we're not worthy? Guess what? We're not! But He is! When we surrender, we find God waiting to embrace us and draw us back into His loving arms. He never runs out of forgiveness for us—we just have to ask. And no matter how low we might feel, there is grace to lift us up.

I love hearing from readers, so please join my newsletter at www.shareestover.com!

Blessings to you,
Sharee Stover